LINDSAY A. MARCUM

Just Below the Surface

First published by Sugarloaf Publishing 2023

Copyright © 2023 by Lindsay A. Marcum

All rights reserved. No part of this publication may be reproduced, stored or transmitted in any form or by any means, electronic, mechanical, photocopying, recording, scanning, or otherwise without written permission from the publisher. It is illegal to copy this book, post it to a website, or distribute it by any other means without permission.

This novel is entirely a work of fiction. The names, characters and incidents portrayed in it are the work of the author's imagination. Any resemblance to actual persons, living or dead, events or localities is entirely coincidental.

Second edition

Editing by Erica Howard

This book was professionally typeset on Reedsy. Find out more at reedsy.com

For my family.
And for all the little girls who scribble on notepads and dream of becoming writers someday.
I thank God for the talent He has given. I want to use it for His glory.

Chapter 1

My hand shakes slightly as I lift my fist to knock on the huge brown door. I never thought a door could give the impression of being cold and unwelcoming. I was wrong. This door seems to scream, Go away! And don't even think about coming back!

I swallow hard and knock anyway, five quick, firm raps. *Lord, I can't unknock now! Is this really what You planned for me?* I know I shouldn't question God's plans, but somehow, I have a hard time believing that this is—

The big brown door swings open and a middle-aged woman with an expression that could crack granite looks me up and down. "Can I help you?" Her voice isn't much softer than her expression.

"I-I..." I begin.

"What is it?" she snaps. Patience doesn't seem to be her strongest attribute.

"I'm here to see Mr. Anderson," I say with all the confidence I can muster.

"Do you have an appointment?"

"Of course," I say, nearly chuckling. It's as if she thinks I'm stupid enough to come without one.

She's not amused, but steps back and gestures for me to come in.

I step over the threshold into a large foyer and freeze. I mean, I actually feel like I'm frozen. It's got to be no more than 60 degrees in here, and the atmosphere is just as unwelcoming as the outside. The floor is marble. Not the shiny, trendy marble with cute little sparkly specks in it, no. This is cold, flat black marble. The walls are gray. Just a flat gray that almost looks like white gone dingy. And the most boring artwork adorns the walls. I shudder. I can't imagine living here, let alone running a company out of this massive home. I'll take my 600 square foot apartment that's warm and cozy over this any day.

The woman, who introduces herself as Mrs. Joy, (I know, a fitting name for such a pleasant character, right?) beckons me to follow her down an undecorated hallway to the right. We pass a few doors, then head up some stairs. At the top left, there's another door, this one dark gray, labeled *Merrick Anderson*.

Mrs. Joy gives two sharp knocks and then twists the door open. Popping her head in, she says, "Mr. Anderson, I believe your next interview is here. A Miss…" She turns quickly to me, giving me a look that says it's my fault she forgot to ask my name.

"Billie Sterling."

She gives me an odd look before turning back to her employer. "Miss Billie Sterling. Shall I send her in?"

"Give me a moment," a deep voice answers from inside.

Is he… *irritated*?

Mrs. Joy pulls the door closed and says, "He'll call you in when he's ready." She walks away with quick footsteps, leaving me to stand here and… wait.

I try to ignore the nerves and sweaty palms as I clutch my resume and some other important papers I have stuffed in a folder. *Why am I here again? Oh yes. I desperately need a job. THIS job.* I say a quick prayer for the hundredth time that everything goes smoothly and I won't embarrass myself.

I wish I had a mirror to check my appearance one more time. I look down to make sure no lint has attached itself to my navy pencil skirt, and double check that my white blouse is neatly tucked in. I reach up, smoothing my hair back toward my sleek ponytail. I know I'm dressed plainly today, but I don't want to give any impressions other than I'm here to get a job, and I

Chapter 1

take myself seriously.

I finish examining myself just as I hear that deep voice again from inside say, "Come in, Miss Sterling."

I swallow hard, dry my palm on my skirt, and twist the doorknob.

I don't know what I expect to see when I walk in, but the scene before me is not it. How did someone so messy get to be so successful?

There are untidy stacks of papers everywhere. There are shelves for organization, yet nothing seems to be organized. And there are sticky notes. Everywhere.

My eyes must be huge because Mr. Anderson's frigid voice interrupts my office analyzation with, "See anything shocking, Miss Sterling?"

My eyes fly to meet his cold brown ones. *Yikes.* I'm not one to listen to rumors, but I'm willing to bet that at least some of them are true.

"I, um, no, nothing, Mr... Sir." Okay, I've officially blown this interview before it has started.

Do I save myself further embarrassment by walking away now?

You need this job, Billie.

Oh. Right.

"Sit down."

I look between two chairs, each facing Mr. Anderson's desk. Oh Lord, what if I choose the wrong one? What is wrong with me? Why am I so—

"Sit *down*, Miss Sterling."

I choose the chair nearest me and sit like an obedient dog. I inwardly groan. I want nothing more than to run out of here, but I convince myself to stay and finish the interview.

Mr. Anderson saves me from my thoughts by getting straight to the point, asking, "What is it that made you apply for this position, Miss Sterling?"

Nice to meet you, too. I fight the urge to roll my eyes. This isn't going as well as I'd hoped.

I take a breath. "To be honest, Mr. Anderson, the salary is why I applied for this job. No other jobs I've found offer the pay and benefits that you offer."

"You're here for the money?" he asks as one eyebrow lifts.

"Yes," I answer truthfully.

He stares at me for a moment, not saying a word. For the first time I take a moment to notice his looks. I can't tell how tall he is while he's sitting behind his desk, but he doesn't appear to be a short man. His dark hair is short and neat—the haircut of a man who has no time to bother with trendy hairstyles and fashion. It screams simple and practical. Thanks to a little research before my interview, I know that he's just celebrated his 30th birthday. Well, *celebrated* may be the wrong word. Rumor has it that he forbade his family to throw him a 30th birthday party, insisting it would be a waste of time and money. He most likely let the day pass while sitting in this office, making more of a mess. Inwardly, I laugh at my own thoughts.

"Well, that's refreshing."

I stare at him, blinking.

"Your honesty, Miss Sterling. No one ever admits that they want the generous salary. They always tell me some story about it being a privilege to work for me, or they can't wait to learn from me, or some nonsense like that." He scoffs. "As if I care that they *like* me. I detest when people become bumbling fools trying to flatter and impress me. I just want someone capable of doing their job."

I don't know how to answer this, or even if I'm supposed to.

I shouldn't have worried. He continues.

"Resume, Miss Sterling?" He holds out his hand.

"Of course," I say quickly, and thumb through the papers in my folder. I pull out my resume and, to my horror, all the other papers slide out with it and fall to the floor in that little floating motion paper is known for. I look up at my interviewer, my face heating.

"Sorry," I mumble. "Hang on, just let me…"

I scoop up the papers quickly and tuck them back in my folder. I hand over the resume.

My eyes meet Mr. Anderson's icy ones and I recognize the look. Annoyance. I sigh softly. There's no saving me now.

I sit in awkward silence as Mr. Anderson looks over my resume, his face stony. *Geez, would it kill a man to smile?* Of course, I don't express my thoughts outwardly, because, well, truth be told, I'm slightly intimidated by the large man sitting on the other side of the disheveled desk. Did I say slightly? I meant extremely. He looks as if at any given moment he's going to jump up from his desk with a Hulk-like growl and toss me out the window for wasting his time.

"You're hired."

"What?"

"You're hired," he repeats, his eyes still on my resume. "Can you start in the morning?"

"Yes!" I say, a little too enthusiastically. Oh well, I'm not too worried about embarrassing myself anymore… I got the job!

After realizing I'm probably wearing the stupidest of silly grins, I stand, composing myself.

"Thank you for this opportunity, Mr. Anderson. You won't be sorry." I hold my hand out to shake his.

He stands for the first time and I tip my head up. *Whoa, he's tall!*

He grips my hand a little too hard. "I certainly hope that's the case, Miss Sterling."

I gulp. Oh boy. Something tells me there's no room for error here…

Mr. Anderson tells me what paperwork I need to get from Mrs. Joy on my way out, and what time he expects me tomorrow. I plan on being early. I leave his office not quite believing what just happened. I collect my paperwork from the delightful Mrs. Joy, who shows a bit of surprise when I tell her I've been hired, and slip out the front door, closing it gently behind me. I lean my back against the door for a moment before heading home. I smile to myself, then I look up and whisper, *"Thank You."*

I can hardly believe it. I'm Merrick Anderson's new assistant.

I suddenly frown, and my pulse races. "Oh my gosh," I say out loud to no one. "I'm Merrick Anderson's new assistant!"

If the rumors are true, I have quite an experience ahead of me.

Chapter 2

I'm up seven minutes before my alarm sounds. I'm to start at 8:00, but I want to make a good impression on my first day, so I mean to be there at 7:45. I make my way into the kitchen and start my coffee.

Lord, I don't know exactly what I'm getting into, I pray. *I just know that I need Your guidance.*

I continue to spend some time with my Heavenly Father as I sip my first cup of coffee. After a short while, I gather my clothes and shower.

I decide to wear my hair down today. I figure it will give me some warmth against the arctic air in my new boss's office. I'm not sure if he turns off the heat, or if his presence alone is the reason for the chill. I shrug, and finish blow-drying my medium length, medium brown hair.

Exciting, I know. But that's me, Billie Sterling, plain and mediocre. Oh, I'm not feeling sorry for myself. In fact, I've never minded blending in. In school I was never popular, but neither was I unpopular. I had a small group of friends and stayed focused on my studies.

I actually *liked* learning. I was one of the few kids who was slightly disappointed when summer vacation arrived. School gave me something to do. I lived with my dad and he worked every day, even most Saturdays. So, I spent a lot of time at home. Alone. At least in school I got to be with people and keep busy.

Why was I alone so much, you ask? Well, it's simple. When your mom

Chapter 2

passes away when you're still a baby, you have no siblings, and your father never remarries, well, there's not much in the way of family to speak of. But I had my dad, and that was all I needed.

Thinking about my dad makes me glance at my watch, and I realize that if I don't leave soon, I won't be able to see him before work. I fill my to-go cup with fresh coffee and creamer, grab my keys, purse, and completed paperwork and lock myself out.

Then I walk three steps and knock softly on the door. "Dad? Are you up?" My voice is quiet.

He answers right away, telling me to come in. I use my extra key to his apartment and let myself in. He's lying on the couch with the old, tattered afghan my grandma made forty-something years ago. It's an ugly shade of green, trimmed with brown and yellow. It's hideous, but my dad loves it.

"Hey, Pumpkin."

I smile at my childhood nickname that he uses even though I'm 27 years old.

"Hi, Dad." I make my way over to him and plant a kiss on his temple. "Have you eaten?"

"Yeah."

I glance at the coffee table littered with prescription bottles. "Taken your meds?"

"Just about to."

I know by heart what he takes, so I start popping the caps off, getting his medication ready for him.

"Listen," I begin. "With this new job, I won't be able to take you on Fridays to your appointments. Can you make other arrangements?" I set the last bottle down and hand him the pills.

He pops them all in at once and takes a huge gulp of water from a bottle he keeps near him. Swallowing, he says, "Already got it covered. Chuck will be taking me."

"Oh, good! Be sure to thank him for me."

Chuck is a retired naval officer who lives in our building. He lost his wife about seven months ago, and he's been keeping himself busy by sharing the load of my sick father with me. He's really been an answer to prayer.

"Dad, I gotta run—I can't be late. Is there anything you need before I go?"

He shakes his head and smiles. "Not a thing, Pumpkin. I got a collection of Don Knotts movies and some junk food I probably shouldn't be eating." We both laugh. "If I have an emergency, I'll call Chuck."

"You can always text me," I say. "I'll answer on my break."

He tries joking with me. "Are you sure the Ice King will let you *have* a break?" He grins.

I make my way to the door, preparing to lock it behind me. "Honestly, Dad, after meeting with him yesterday, I don't think he'll be that bad! I think the rumors about him are greatly exaggerated."

* * *

I was wrong. Oh, how wrong I was.

I show up seventeen minutes early, and he scowls at me as I come through the door. He makes a production out of glancing at his watch, as if to check if I really had made it on time.

"Good morning, Mr. Anderson," I say in my best chipper voice, trying to mask my nerves. *Confidence, Billie*, I tell myself. *He can probably smell your fear.* I suppress a giggle at the ridiculous thought, and that brings another scowl from my new boss. I clear my throat and get myself under control. Clearly, this is no place for fun.

"Good morning, Miss Sterling. After you've settled at your desk, I'll need you to make some coffee."

Um.

"Yes, sir. Just show me to my office, and I'll get right to it."

"You'll be there, of course." My employer points across the room to a shabby desk that's in need of a thorough scrub down.

Oh, no, no, nonono.

"Er, here, with you?" I manage to squeak out. I thought I'd have a private place to work.

"Are you not my assistant, Miss Sterling?"

Chapter 2

"I... yes, of course," I say, as I try to keep my composure. "I just thought, well, I thought I'd have an office of my own."

"Well, that makes no sense. I need you here, with me."

He says it so matter-of-factly, I nearly forget that he terrifies me and almost agree with him.

He glances at his watch again, to prove a point about wasting time, I'm sure, and turns back to his laptop.

I hurry over to my "new" desk and get a closer look. It's so covered in dust, I wonder when it was that someone last occupied it. I glance around the room, looking for something. I spot a canister of disinfecting wipes on one of the shelves. That'll have to do.

I walk over to the shelf and pick up the canister. "May I use these?" I don't want to assume.

Mr. Anderson never looks up from his screen as he nods.

Seriously? He can't spare a half second to answer me?

"Thanks," I mumble as I walk back to my desk.

It takes nearly the entire can of wipes to get the dust off my desk, but it smells like oranges now, so I don't really mind.

I hate to interrupt him, but I need to know where the coffee is. "Uh, Mr. Anderson... sir?"

He turns to me. "Do you think you could possibly sound a little less like a scared rabbit, and more like a confident assistant? What is it you need, Miss Sterling?"

My face flames as I try to process what he just said to me. *The nerve!* Doesn't he realize that this is my first day and I know nothing? Could he at least *try* to understand the nerves that accompany first days at a new place, with a new boss?

I nearly laugh as I answer my own question. *Of course he doesn't. He's been his own boss since he graduated college and started his own business. He sweats confidence.*

I swallow and lift my chin slightly, trying not to let his comment bother me. "Where is the coffee?"

He looks at me as if it should be obvious. "In the kitchen." He turns back to his screen and begins typing.

I turn to walk out of the office, prepared to find my way around by myself, when I hear, "Two sugars, one cream."

I grit my teeth and resist the urge to roll my eyes. "Yes, sir," I say sweetly as I leave. I cannot get out of the room fast enough.

* * *

I find the kitchen without a problem. As I walk in, I mutter, "He's impossible!" and head to the coffee pot.

"Well, now, Miss Sterling, is it really as bad as all that?"

I whirl around to face Mrs. Joy.

My hand flies to my chest and I say, "Mrs. Joy! I didn't realize you were in here."

"Clearly."

"I'm so sorry, I was just—"

"Stating the truth?"

Um.

"Ma'am?"

"Oh, go on with you." She waves her hand dismissively. "I've been Merrick's housekeeper for six years. I ought to know a bit about how impossible he can be."

I risk a smile at the lady I clearly misread yesterday. Stern, yes. Uptight, maybe. But definitely not the old biddy I assumed her to be. I mentally chastise myself for the horrible thought toward Mrs. Joy.

She almost returns my smile—I swear I see the corner of her mouth twitch in a very upward fashion—and she opens a cupboard above her head. "I assume he wants his coffee?"

I peek into the cupboard that holds the bag of Honduran coffee, filters, and sugar packets. I give Mrs. Joy a grateful look. "Thank you," I say.

She's already at the fridge, pulling out a bowl of individual hazelnut creamers. "You're welcome," she says before handing me the creamer. "He likes these."

Chapter 2

I begin making the coffee when a thought occurs to me. I can ask *her!* I flip the coffee pot to "on" and turn to face Mrs. Joy, who is now organizing some things in the pantry.

"May I ask you a question, ma'am? It's kind of... well, it's a little embarrassing, on my part."

"'Mrs. Joy' is fine, no more of this 'ma'am' stuff. And ask away. I've got kids and grandkids, so nothing shocks me."

I giggle at her attempt at humor, then plow forward with my question. "Um, what does Mr. Anderson actually do? I was so desperate for a job, and when I saw 'Assistant Needed' online, I kind of forgot to find out what I'm assisting."

I swear I haven't grown another head, but Mrs. Joy looks at me as though I have. "You don't know what Merrick does?" She blinks, clearly trying to process my stupidity. At least that's what it looks like.

I feel like a jerk for asking. *I should know this!*

When I don't say anything, Mrs. Joy takes pity on me and answers my question. "He plans events."

My mouth drops open in the most unladylike way. "He's... an *event planner?*" My mind instantly conjures up pictures of six-foot-something Mr. Anderson dressed as a clown in front of a dozen obnoxious five-year-olds, and I can't stifle my giggle.

Mrs. Joy frowns. The coffee is ready, and I reach for a mug to prepare Mr. Anderson's cup.

"It's not the kind of event planner you're thinking of, Miss Sterling. He plans large social events, many of which are covered in the papers and online."

My mouth forms an "o" as I begin to understand. Of course. He didn't get rich by throwing birthday parties for toddlers.

"Remember last month, when the governor hosted the banquet that raised over $800,000 for Alzheimer's research?"

I stop stirring the coffee and look up at her. "Yeah?"

She smiles and nods her head.

"No. Way."

She chuckles. "Yes. From beginning to end."

"But… a *charity event*? That seems so…" I shake my head, unable to find the word.

"Be careful when you listen to rumors, Miss Sterling." She walks out of the kitchen.

I stand there for a moment, and then I realize that my boss most likely prefers his coffee hot. I quickly clean up the small mess I've made and head upstairs, thinking that I really have no idea what kind of man Mr. Anderson truly is.

Chapter 3

I open the door and find Mr. Anderson on the phone, so I silently set his cup down to the left of him. Without looking at me, he picks it up and sets it to his right. That's it. No nod, no mouthed *"Thank you."* I ignore the little voice inside telling me to shout, *"You're welcome!"* out of spite, and walk over to my desk.

I just now realize that I have no chair.

I wait a full four minutes before my boss hangs up. I watch as he takes a sip of his coffee and sets it back down. When he doesn't comment that it's horrible, I assume it's satisfactory. He turns to me.

"Is there a problem, Miss Sterling?" he asks when he sees me standing there, staring.

"Yes. I don't have a chair."

"Oh." He stands and opens a door that I assume is a closet and disappears for a few moments. I hear a scuffling noise, and he reappears holding an old black swivel chair in one hand. He walks to my desk and sets it down.

How gracious.

He heads back to the closet. I wonder what he's doing now.

I wait no more than a few seconds, and Mr. Anderson returns, holding an old office phone. He walks around to the side of my desk nearest the wall, and crouches down. I watch as he plugs the phone into the jack then sets it on my desk.

"I'll need you to start answering the phone."

"Of course," I say. I wait.

"Miss Sterling, do you have a question?" His face remains stone.

"Uh, I have a million."

"Excuse me?"

"Pardon me, Mr. Anderson, but I was under the assumption that this job requires more of me than making coffee and answering the phone. You've seen my resume. I'm capable of much more."

He's quiet for a moment, then gives a curt nod. "You're right. I suppose I did hire you for a reason." He scrubs his hand over his face and turns back to his desk. He sits, then turns his chair to me.

I take that moment to sit myself, and almost yelp as I nearly fall out of the chair. I jump to a standing position and grab the back of the chair and shake it. It wiggles and rattles like no desk chair should. I can't stop myself from sending a glare my employer's way.

"Oh, I guess I didn't realize..." Mr. Anderson's voice trails off.

Could he be... *embarrassed?*

I take pity on him and ask, "Have you ever had an assistant before, Mr. Anderson?"

He scowls as if I've offended him with the question. But he looks up and says, "Truthfully, no. I've taken care of everything myself since starting M.A. Planning. Mrs. Joy recently talked me into advertising for an assistant. She insists I work myself too hard." He scoffs.

I walk over to his desk and lean on it with my hand. I remember what he said about people trying to impress him, so I ask, "How many people did you interview before me?"

"About forty."

Forty?

The next question is out of my mouth before I have time to decide if it's appropriate to ask.

"Why did you hire *me?*"

"I liked your honesty," he states simply.

Um.

Chapter 3

I decide that it doesn't really matter *why* he hired me, just that he did. I look at him and sigh.

"Well, I guess in a way, we're both new."

"I suppose so, Miss Sterling." His face never softens.

I decide to take initiative. "Can I use one of these?" I point to the two chairs facing his desk.

Saying nothing, he holds out his hand as if to say, *be my guest.*

I drag one of the square chairs to my desk and roll the broken one toward the door. "Um, this can probably go to the trash."

I get one nod.

I sit down on the much more comfortable chair but notice it's a little short for my desk. I don't mention it, though. I look around the room, once again taking in all the clutter.

"Would you like me to organize this room a bit?" I ask.

He swivels in his chair to face me. And stares.

Oh Lord. When is he going to stop shooting me daggers with his eyes? I feel like more of an annoyance than an assistant.

Finally, he says, "I guess this office *could* use a bit of tidying up."

That's the understatement of the year. I say nothing, though, because I'm just excited to have something to do.

I'm deciding where to start, and I notice Mr. Anderson has already gone back to his laptop and is reading something intently. Oh, well. I sigh. So much for small talk.

I choose a shelf to start with and push my sleeves up.

※ ※ ※

It's a quarter to twelve when I finish. With the *first* shelf. Receipts are in one pile, papers to be filed in another, and about three hundred sticky notes fill a small box. I grin. The things written on some of them are almost… cute. There are more than a few that say, *call mom.*

Other notes have phone numbers, some with names, some without.

I pick up what I think is just a piece of cardstock. But when I turn it over, I see that it's an old photo glued to paper. I immediately recognize the brown eyes and hair. It's Mr. Anderson. And he's about twelve years old.

The next thing I realize is that he's standing in a church. And the biggest shocker? *He's smiling.*

Oh, my day has just gotten a little brighter. I smile to myself, prepared to tease my employer a bit about the old photo.

"So, that mouth *does* turn in both directions," I say, flashing the picture in front of him.

He looks at what I'm holding in my hand, and his face darkens. "I don't have time for ridiculous small talk and banter, Miss Sterling." His long arm reaches to me and snatches the photo. He drops it in the garbage can next to his desk and turns back to his computer.

I turn around, heading back to the shelf. *Okay. No sense of humor,* I pretend to write on an imaginary list. I can't guess if he's irritated at me for trying to joke with him or upset at the photo I found. Either way, as I go back to my organizing, I can't stop thinking about Mr. Anderson standing in a church. *Looking happy to be there.*

* * *

Around one o'clock, I realize I'm starving. I could also use a trip to the restroom. I turn to Mr. Anderson, ready to hesitate in asking for a break, when I remember his earlier words. *Scared rabbit...* I lift my chin and simply blurt out, "I'm taking my lunch break."

"Fine."

That was easy.

"Um," I start. "Do you need me to bring you back anything?"

He stares up at me, as if the thought had never occurred to him. After a moment, he pulls a twenty from his wallet and hands it to me. "I'll call Clark's Burgers in about forty-five minutes and order. You can just bring it back with you."

"Okay," I say, taking the bill. "See you in an hour."

He says nothing as I walk out the door.

Chapter 3

A few moments later I get in my little black Fiesta and I sit there for a moment, staring at the steering wheel. *Can I do this? Can I come in every day and work with someone so... so...* I can't even think of an adequate word to describe Mr. Anderson. I know my thoughts toward him throughout the morning haven't been very positive. On more than one occasion, I bit my tongue when receiving a sharp comment from him. *But oh, I had such clever comebacks,* I think, smiling.

I decide to eat at Clark's, since I'll be picking up food to bring back anyway. I start to drive off when a thought hits me. *I haven't even stopped to pray for or about him.*

I'm sorry, Lord, I pray sincerely. *I've just been caught up in his coldness and haven't stopped to think that maybe You have me there for a reason. Please help me navigate my way through this, and not do anything stupid.*

I add that last part in my prayer, because, well, lately I'm *always* doing something stupid. At least it seems that way. I groan as I remember my outburst in my father's doctor's office when I thought the nurse gave him the wrong instructions. Turns out, his doctor was trying a new treatment, and I sort of jumped to conclusions. Oops. *I need some serious work, Lord.*

As I pull in the lot and look for an empty parking space, I remember something else. The picture of Mr. Anderson in church. I grin. Maybe there *is* a reason I'm here.

***

I hurry back with Mr. Anderson's lunch, terrified it will be cold and I'll get an earful. I enter the office and shut the door behind me. I walk to his desk, but he's not there. I set the bag of food down, lay his change right beside it, and get back to my shelf organizing.

A moment later, Mr. Anderson comes in the door with a fresh cup of coffee and a water bottle. He barely glances my way before sitting at his desk and digging into the bag.

Make sure to chew, I think, rolling my eyes.

Out of the corner of my eye, I see him pick up the receipt and count his change.

You've got to be kidding me! Is he serious?

Then I remember that he's only known me about twenty-four hours, and I try not to take offense. After all, he *does* seem the type that doesn't trust many people. I go back to my work.

After about twenty minutes, I realize that I have stacks of papers and receipts that need to be filed, but there's no filing cabinet. I turn to Mr. Anderson, ready to ask him where I can find one, and I see he's on the phone.

Take some initiative, Billie. He wants confidence and competence.

I stand from the place I'd been sitting while going through trash—er—I mean, *papers*, and glance at the door to the mysterious room wherein my boss found my treasure of an office chair. Hmm. I slip past him, and he never glances my way. I slowly turn the knob, bracing myself for any comments I may receive if he's not happy about me coming in here.

Nothing.

Certain now that it's not a dungeon hiding former disobedient assistants, I open the door and step inside. It's dusty and smells like an old library. Then I see why. There are shelves of books. Hundreds of books. The room is about 12'x15', and at least half the space is taken by book shelves. I see a few old (we're talking 1990s) office supplies, and a desk in worse shape than mine. Now I know where the chair came from. I shake my head.

There. I spot a black two-drawer filing cabinet that looks to be in decent shape. I pray it's empty. I walk over and pull the drawers open, one at a time. They're not empty, but there are only a few papers and files. Not too bad. I pull everything out and stack it on a shelf where there's a little space.

Then I grab the sides and pull. It's heavy but manageable. It slides easily across the floor, so I get behind it and push it to the door. I open the door quietly, in case Mr. Anderson is still on the phone. I turn, holding the door open with my backside as I pull the filing cabinet through. Once I have it halfway in the office, I change positions and push it the rest of the way.

I get it to a corner where I think it will fit nicely, and when I turn to grab some stack of papers to file, I catch my boss watching me. I can't begin to know what he's thinking, because it seems he only has one look—indifferent.

Chapter 3

He goes back to his computer screen and I grab my stacks of papers.

Mr. Anderson says very little the rest of the afternoon. I answer the phone a few times, and he gives me a few errands to run. In between the errands and phone calls, I bulldoze through his mess, organizing and filing.

When the day ends at 5:00, I'm exhausted and ready to leave. And would you like to hear the end-of-my-first-day encouraging words from my employer?

"See you tomorrow."

Chapter 4

I fall into bed at 9:40. I have a feeling that my new job is going to be mentally exhausting as well as physically. I go over the day in my mind and wonder if there's anything I could've done differently.

I hear a *ding* and check my phone. *You still up?? Call me!!*

It's a text from my cousin Anne. My dad must've told her about my first day. I groan and hit the call button. She answers so quickly I laugh.

"Billie? Oh. My. Word. Why didn't you tell me you're working for *Merrick Anderson*? Is he as horrible as they say?"

"Hi Anne. I'm fine, thanks for asking."

"Billie. I'm serious! How did you get a job working for *him*?"

Anne has always been straightforward, especially with me. We're only two months apart, so growing up we hit all the major milestones together. The only bad part was she lived with her mom (my dad's sister) over an hour away, so much of our time spent was on the phone and not in person. But we're still as close as ever.

I shrug, even though she can't see me. "I saw online that he was looking for an assistant, so I applied. I got an email that night saying I had an interview two days later. I went, he hired me." I pause. "It pays *really* well."

"This is literally the most exciting thing that has happened to either one of us," she breathes, and I roll my eyes at her dramatics.

"So…" she begins.

Chapter 4

"So, what?"

I can hear the smile in her voice as she asks, "Is he as handsome as he is horrible?"

"Anne!"

She laughs. "Well, if you have to deal with his awful personality, he may as well be nice to look at."

I huff. "Be serious. You know how I feel about that."

"I know, I know." She takes on a proper lady tone and says, *"Looks don't make the man. Good character does."* She laughs.

"It's true!" I insist. "I've found many men attractive after I get to know them, even if I didn't at first. And vice versa."

"Uuugggghhhh, you're so *practical*," she teases.

"One of us has to be," I say with a smile.

We chat for a few minutes and I tell her about my first day. She eats it up like a woman starved. Finally, we start winding down the conversation, and she gets quiet.

"What are you thinking?" I ask.

"Oh, nothing important," she says. "Just that you still haven't answered my question."

Against my better judgment, I ask, "What question?"

"Do you find him attractive?"

"Good night, Anne." I end the call, laughing.

***

Today is Friday, and as I walk into the office for my second day, I can't help but be grateful that the weekend is almost here. I plan on spending some much-needed time with my dad.

I don't have time to think about that, though, because I'm greeted by my boss, who has his jacket and keys in his hand.

"Forget the coffee today, Miss Sterling. We can grab some on the way."

"Good morning," I make sure to start with. "On the way, sir?"

"I have a meeting today. Or rather, *we* have a meeting." He pulls a binder from the top drawer of his desk and hands it to me. "Do you have a pen?"

I pat my purse. "Always."

"Good." He walks toward the door. I follow.

On our way out, he simply tells Mrs. Joy, "I'll be back."

She nods and shoots me a grin. Obviously, she's used to his nearly nonexistent communication skills.

I follow him to his six-car garage and my eyes go wide. Why does one man need *three* vehicles? He walks up to a black SUV and hits the unlock button on his key fob. I assume this is the one we're taking so I climb in the passenger seat.

He opens the back door and pulls out a briefcase. Then he looks at me. "Miss Sterling, we're not taking this."

I feel my cheeks heat as I slip out of the car and close the door. "Oh, I assumed—"

"Exactly." He walks to the silver Mercedes and gestures for me to get in.

I get in and buckle my seat belt, wishing I didn't have to be sitting so close to him for the next—well, I don't know how long because I have no idea where we're going.

He backs out of the driveway and drives in silence the first few minutes. No light conversation, no music. Just awkward silence. I spot my favorite local coffee shop, Sam's, but before I can mention it, he hits his blinker. I turn to my window so he doesn't see me smile.

He parks and we walk into the little shop. When we step inside I breathe deeply. Coffee shops are at the top of my list of favorite smells. Fresh bread and muffins peeking out from behind the glass counter make my mouth water. But I already know I'm going to choose my favorite—an everything bagel, double toasted with extra chive cream cheese.

I stand behind my boss, who is obviously eager to order. *So much for ladies first.* I can't keep myself from rolling my eyes just slightly.

He orders enough for three people, then steps aside to wait for his food. I step up to the counter and order my bagel and coffee. I swipe my debit card, grab my receipt, and go to stand next to him.

He says nothing. He doesn't even acknowledge me standing next to him. I hate that my face heats up. *Is he embarrassed to be here with me?* I say nothing, though, and continue to wait for my order.

Mr. Anderson gets his food, and I half expect him to walk out and leave me there. But he doesn't. Instead, he waits—quietly, of course. When I grab my coffee and bag, he turns to leave and I follow him out.

We get into the car, and I just can't take the silence anymore.

"So, where are we going?" I ask.

"Battle Creek."

"That's over an hour away!"

"So it is."

I fold my arms in front of me. It's chilly in his car. *No surprise there.*

"What time is the meeting?"

"Ten."

I glance at the clock. 8:32. *Great. Over an hour of stone-cold silence or one-word answers. Yay, me.*

For lack of something better to do while I eat my bagel, I flip open the binder he gave me back in the office. I see a paper titled: *Battle Creek Military Ball.* My eyebrows raise.

"*You* are planning a *ball*?" I ask, not bothering to hide my smile.

He swallows the last bite of his first muffin. "Is there something humorous about that, Miss Sterling?"

"Well…" I begin, "a little."

"What could possibly be funny about arranging an event for our men and women in uniform?"

I shift slightly in my seat to get a better look at him. I try to keep my voice light as I say, "It just doesn't seem like something—"

He cuts me off. "You've known me for two days, Miss Sterling. How in the world could you possibly know what kinds of things I like to do or not do?" His voice is icy, and I swear the temperature drops a few degrees in the car.

"I didn't mean—"

"I couldn't care less what you meant." His eyes never leave the road. "You should never give opinions on things you know nothing about."

Whoa. This guy's wound tighter than a tension spring!

I quickly decide that awkward silence is better than a conversation with an iceberg. I turn back to the front. I finish my bagel and pull my phone from my purse. I sip my coffee as I scroll through my social media. Anne has tagged me in a hilarious meme and I chuckle softly. Out of the corner of my eye, I see my boss glance my way, then turn back to the road ahead of him.

Could he be curious as to what I find funny? I smirk. *Let him wonder.*

I keep scrolling, and a beautiful scenic picture catches my eye. Across the top is written, *"I will give you a new heart, and I will put a new spirit in you. I will take out your stony, stubborn heart and give you a tender, responsive heart."* Ezekiel 36:26

My breath catches in my throat. I immediately think of my employer. Could God really change someone that hardened? I know the answer. Worse people than Mr. Anderson have come to know the Lord and have completely changed. It's just hard to picture when you're face to face with the impossible.

I pray silently. *Let me show Your love to him, Father. And please, help me to not take his words and actions personally, but to see the bigger picture. Help me to see him through Your eyes.*

I'm ready to close out the app when I see another post. My hand flies to my mouth when I see Mr. Anderson, and he looks as if he's shouting at someone. It's *not* a great photo. The heading of the picture reads, *Inexorable Merrick Anderson snubs another invitation to host award event...*

I need to click on the link to see more, but I don't. I close out the app and tuck my phone back in my purse. I stare out the window. I can't help but wonder if the media is being unfair to him.

But why doesn't he stand up for himself? I glance in his direction and study his hard, set jawline. He just seems... *bitter*.

We drive the rest of the way in silence, which is fine with me, because I have no idea what to say.

Chapter 5

I park my Fiesta in a pretty great spot. We're at the Waterloo State Park on Portage Lake. It's early October and it's too chilly to enjoy the water, but Dad and I want to make the most out of this Michigan fall weather and enjoy the outdoors.

I grab our cooler from the back as Dad gets out of the car. He's moving a little slower these days, but I don't mind. It's time I get to spend with him, and for that I'm grateful.

"Did you bring an extra blanket?"

He frowns. "I forgot."

"It's okay," I say. "Let me check my trunk."

I walk around to my trunk and hit the button. It pops open and I look inside. I see a gray fleece blanket rolled up, and I grab it.

"Ah. Here we go."

Dad gets cold so easily now, and I'd hate for him to be miserable and not say anything. Because he won't. He'll just sit there and claim he's fine, so he doesn't spoil my time. As if he could.

There's a long, paved pathway down to the beach, where little grills and picnic tables are set up. I've got my eye on one that's not too close to the water. It takes us almost ten minutes to reach it and Dad apologizes.

"There's nothing to be sorry for," I say. "But if you feel that bad, *you* can grill the burgers."

He laughs, and I'm glad. I don't want him feeling bad on this trip.

We get settled and get the grill fired up, which is nice because it adds a little warmth to our spot. Dad has already wrapped the fleece blanket around his shoulders.

"So," he begins, as he twists the cap off a bottle of water. "Tell me how it's going."

I give him a skeptical look. "Life in general? Or do you have a specific topic in mind?"

He smiles and shrugs. "I just want to know how the past two days have gone."

"I knew it!" I laugh. "You're as bad as Anne!"

He tries his best to look innocent, but there's a gleam in his eye as he says, "Tell me about this meeting you mentioned." He pops a chip into his mouth.

"Well," I say, reaching past him to grab my own handful of chips. "I was a little surprised, I guess."

"How so?"

"It's weird, Dad. He hired me, but it's like he doesn't want me to be there. He's quiet to the point of being rude, and it's like he doesn't know how to communicate in a civilized manner with me. But then, at the meeting, he turned into this charming version of Merrick Anderson. He was so confident and prepared. At one point, he actually seemed… *nice*."

My dad laughs. "Sounds like a good businessman."

"I hate to admit it, but he's an *incredible* businessman." I crunch a chip and swallow. "You should have seen his list of contacts and connections. Any time they questioned him about his plans, he had several names and companies to present to them. It's like he knows everyone, and people are just lined up to work with him."

"So, what's the problem with that? It sounds like you work for a great man and great company."

I take a sip of my iced tea before answering. "I don't know. Nothing, I guess. It's just that he clearly *needs* an assistant. But he acts like he doesn't want me there."

My dad looks at me thoughtfully. "I think it'll work out," he says knowingly.

Chapter 5

"How can you know?"

He looks at me for a moment and then says, "I don't think it's that he doesn't want you there, Billie. I think the issue might be that he doesn't *want* to want you there."

***

I get my dad settled in for the night before I walk next door to my own apartment. I'm still thinking about his comment as I climb into bed. And I'm still not sure what he meant by it.

I set my alarm for early the next morning, giving me enough time to get myself ready for church, then see if Dad needs any help. That's if he's feeling up to going. He gets nervous around big crowds because his immune system is basically non-existent right now. I can't blame him. Every head cold to him is like raging influenza.

I roll over, pulling my covers snug around me, and face the window. My curtain is slightly crooked, parting and giving me a perfect view of the moon. I look up at it and talk to its Creator. I end my prayer with, *Lord, whatever Mr. Anderson is facing, let him know You're there. Let him see that Your love is unlike any person's, in that it's perfect. We don't earn it, and we can't lose it. Help me show him Your love, Lord.*

I drift off to sleep knowing my work situation is out of my hands, and into much more capable ones.

***

It's Monday morning and I set Mr. Anderson's coffee cup down. To his *right*. He doesn't notice the extra effort I make, of course. He just picks it up and takes a sip. I roll my eyes and walk to my desk.

I still have some organizing left to do because we were gone most of Friday. I reach down and grab the box on the floor to the right of my desk and sit down to go through it. The sticky notes. I want to thin the herd a bit, but who am I to say which ones are important?

I decide to organize by category. Phone numbers with names in one stack, without names in another. Random reminder notes in one stack, mom notes in another, and so on.

Once I get them sorted by category, I look through each stack to see if there are duplicates. There are. *A lot.* I get rid of all the unnecessary extras and see that I've made quite a dent. *Now we're getting somewhere.*

Next, I look for any with dates on them and separate those by past and future. Then a note catches my eye.

Margaret's Bday—10/11

That's tomorrow.

I check to make sure Mr. Anderson is not on a phone call before approaching his desk. "Um, sir?" I lay the sticky note in front of him. "I thought this might be important."

He turns from his computer screen and glances at the note.

"It is."

He picks it up and sticks it to the side of his screen. He looks up at me standing over him as if to say, *anything else?*

I don't hold my breath waiting for a thank you. I simply turn back to my desk and get back to work. But that doesn't stop me from thinking, *I don't know who this Margaret is, but perhaps I should've thrown the note away and let him feel her wrath for forgetting her birthday.*

I unashamedly smile at the thought.

A moment later, I can't help overhearing my boss's phone conversation. He's ordering flowers. For tomorrow. For a Margaret. A Margaret *Joy.*

Oh! So *that's* her first name! Well, now I'm glad I gave him the note. I wouldn't want Mrs. Joy to miss out on her birthday flowers from her employer.

Immediately I think of my own birthday and wonder if I'll get flowers. I blush at the thought.

Wait, what? Why are you thinking about your boss giving you flowers, Billie? Mrs. Joy has worked for him for years and is probably like a mother figure to him! He's known you less than a week and doesn't even like you. You're not getting flowers!

Chapter 5

I'm thankful my thoughts aren't readable, because I'm pretty sure I'd keel over if Mr. Anderson knew I was thinking about him giving me flowers.

Oh my GOSH, Billie! Think of something else!

I go back to my sticky note mission and put the flowers out of my mind.

* * *

The office is looking pretty good. I've been in the closet room a few times and found some useful things. Some push pins, a few paper clips, an electric pencil sharpener, and a stapler that reminds me of my 4th grade teacher, Mrs. Belcher. That lady used her stapler for *everything*. I remember one day she snagged the arm of her sweater on the corner of the chalkboard and it left a hole. She stapled it closed.

The only thing I haven't tackled is Mr. Anderson's desk. I feel like that space is too personal. I decide to wait for him to ask me to organize it. That way I won't feel like I'm overstepping.

My watch tells me I'm overdue for a break, so I tell Mr. Anderson I'm heading out for lunch.

He lets me know it's fine by saying "Fine."

He has such a way with words, doesn't he?

I offer to bring him back something, but today he declines. He tells me to just bring him a fresh cup of coffee on my way back up.

Hmm. I glance at him before I leave, and he seems to be staring blankly at the screen in front of him, in a daze.

I leave for lunch but can't help wondering what's wrong with him.

* * *

I don't have to wonder for long.

When I get back up to the office an hour later with his fresh coffee, I see Mr. Anderson sitting in the exact position he was in when I left. And he looks miserable.

I walk to his desk and set down his coffee, preparing to ask him if there's anything I can help him with. That's when my hand brushes his and I feel it. He's *hot*.

I gasp softly, and before I think better of it, I reach out and place my hand on his forehead.

After a moment, I realize what I've done, and nearly snatch my hand back. But not before his eyes slide closed and he leans into my touch.

Oh my gosh, he's delirious! That's the only explanation for what just happened.

"Mr. Anderson, sir? Are you alright?"

He looks up at me with glassy eyes and I realize his cheeks are a bright pink. I almost laugh at how much he looks like a little boy.

His hands go up to his throat and he says hoarsely, "My throat hurts a bit."

"Dear Lord, Mr. Anderson, *a bit?* You're burning up!"

"I don't get sick."

"Well, you can *not be sick* later. I'm helping you to bed." I grab his arm and coax him to stand.

"Maybe if I just lie down for a few…" he mumbles, walking toward the door.

"I'll get Mrs. Joy," I offer. "She knows your home as well as you. I'm sure she can get you settled."

He shakes his head. "Margaret is running my errands today. She won't be here until tomorrow." He swallows and grimaces.

"Okay. Then come on."

He doesn't argue as he follows me down the stairs. I don't want to intrude on his privacy by walking in his bedroom, so I lead him to the most comfortable-looking couch in his massive living room.

"Sit down," I say.

He obeys.

I smile, thinking that I could get used to this Mr. Anderson. Well, not the raging fever, most likely has a throat infection Mr. Anderson. The compliant one.

"Where can I find a blanket?" I ask.

He points to the right. "End of the hall. Closet." Swallow. Grimace.

Chapter 5

"Alright, hang on." I walk down the hall to the door that looks to be a closet. I open it and find I'm right. On the top shelf are several extra blankets and pillows. Below those are sets of clean sheets. I grab a navy-blue blanket that looks quite warm, a pillow, and a pillowcase. I head back to the living room.

"Here, sit up for a second, okay?" I notice his eyes are closing.

He leans forward. I quickly drop the pillow into the case and stick it behind him.

"There. Lean back."

Again he obeys, and again his eyes close.

I drop the blanket over him, even though he's still in his dress pants and very starchy shirt and tie.

"Before you go to sleep, sir, can you find your doctor's number for me?"

He pulls his phone from his pocket and scrolls through his contacts. After a moment he hands it to me. I take it, walk to the kitchen, and hit the call button.

I come back to him a few minutes later. "The office said Dr. Blair can see you first thing tomorrow morning. She's booked the rest of the day. Do you want to go to urgent care?"

He shakes his head. "I'll wait."

I take a deep breath and try to think. Mrs. Joy isn't in today. The doctor can't see him until tomorrow. There's only one thing I can think of to do.

I'll have to take care of him.

Chapter 6

Mr. Anderson has closed his eyes again, so I slip out of the living room and head back upstairs. Once in the office, I grab my purse and dig out my phone. I pull up my dad's number and hit *call*.

After about ten seconds he answers. "Hi, Pumpkin."

"Hey, Dad. How are you feeling?"

"It's a good day."

"Good." I smile. That's what I was hoping to hear. "Hey, listen. I won't be home for a while—I'm working late. But even when I get home, I'm not going to be stopping by to see you. I probably will just call you during the next few days."

"Oh?"

I sigh. "Mr. Anderson is really sick, and I've been around him all day. I can't risk passing it to you." I pause. "Plus, I'm staying late because he's alone and I think he could use some help."

"Ever the good Samaritan," my dad jokes.

"Will you be okay?" I ask, unsure.

"Of course, Billie. You know I appreciate your concern, but do what you need to do. I'll see what Chuck is making for dinner and get him to bring me some." We both laugh.

"Thanks, Dad. I love you."

Chapter 6

"Love you, too, Pumpkin. Take care of that boss of yours."

"I will. I'll talk to you later. Call me anytime if it's urgent."

"I know the drill."

I smile as I end the call. Then I head out the door with my jacket and purse. I'm going shopping.

* * *

When I return, I quickly check on my employer. He's out cold. I notice that he's loosened his tie, though. His cheeks are still bright, and I lay my cool hand on his forehead. I don't have a thermometer to check, but I'm willing to bet his temperature is at least 103°.

I head back to the kitchen where I set the bags and begin to go through them. I put the massive bag of popsicles right in the freezer, and set the Kool-Aid canister down on the counter.

I hope he likes cherry. I put the apple juice and chicken thighs in the fridge and leave the veggies on the counter.

I think about calling Mrs. Joy to ask her if she thinks it's alright for me to cook here, but I decide not to. Mr. Anderson is in no position to be angry with me about anything right now. If he decides to throw a fit later, I'll deal with it then.

Right now I need a pot. I glance around. Kitchens are all pretty much the same, right? Well, except for the fact that the one I'm standing in now has about two-thirds more cupboard space than mine, and twice the counter space. Oh, and every major appliance is bigger. I smile. Actually, this is my dream kitchen. This is going to be fun.

I try to rein my excitement in a bit, because, well, my boss is two rooms over as sick as a dog. I can't enjoy myself too much. But I am doing this for him, so I will enjoy his kitchen guilt-free.

After looking through a few of the larger cupboards, I find the pots and pans I need for homemade chicken noodle soup. A few minutes later, I have myself a cutting board, a *great* chef's knife, and some seasonings.

I get to work.

* * *

It's an hour and a half later, and Mr. Anderson's kitchen smells divine. I've checked on him several times, but he hasn't stirred. I clean up my mess and ladle myself a bowl of soup to set aside to cool. Then I grab a coffee cup and ladle in just the broth. I head back to the living room.

"Mr. Anderson, sir?" I say softly.

It takes him a moment, but he opens his eyes. He looks at me, his eyes focusing. "You're still here?" he whispers. His voice is hoarse.

I ignore the irritation I hear and chalk it up to his illness. *Yeah, right. Who am I kidding?*

"You're sick, sir. I figured you could use some soup. Well, the broth, at least. I'm not sure if you could swallow the noodles and chicken." I sit on the edge of the couch and hand him the mug. "Be careful, it's really hot."

He takes the mug of broth and eyes me warily. "You made this?"

"I did."

He looks down at his cup. I can't tell what he's thinking. He just looks tired.

I watch him gently blow on the broth and cautiously take a small sip. He closes his eyes and swallows. Then he looks at me and nods.

What, sir? What are you thinking? Thank you? It's good? What? I hate that he's so unreadable.

"Well," I say. "I know you're feeling pretty bad, but you're in for a treat."

His eyebrow lifts just slightly.

"Drink your broth. I'll be back in a few minutes."

Once back in the kitchen, I start my special drink. It takes me hardly any time to gather a two-quart pitcher and a blender. I add water and Kool-Aid powder to the pitcher and mix it. Then I pour a little into the blender.

I take the apple juice from the fridge and add a little of that, too. Lastly, I grab a handful of popsicles from the freezer and cut them open. I knock them off their sticks right into the blender. I put the lid on and hit the "crushed ice" button. After a few seconds, I pour the icy, reddish-purple liquid into a glass. It smells fruity. I'm satisfied with the drink, but one

Chapter 6

thing's missing. After looking, I find straws in the pantry and stick one in the glass, then head back to the living room.

I take Mr. Anderson's mug. About a quarter of the broth is gone. I set the cup on a coaster on the coffee table. "Here." I hold out the glass to him.

He frowns but takes it.

I hear him whisper, *"What the heck?"*

"Just try it." I wait.

He puts the straw to his lips and takes a drink. I can tell it's hard for him to swallow, but he does.

"What is this?" he asks.

"It's something my dad used to make for me whenever I had a sore throat. I never could eat much but needed liquids. To me, it was like having a slushy."

"But what *is* it?"

"It's..." I hesitate. "Apple juice, popsicles, and..."

His brows go up as if to say, *and?*

"And Kool-Aid."

He stares at me.

I stare back.

"I'm not a child, Miss Sterling."

That's it. I turn and walk back to the kitchen without another word.

I sit down at the counter and eat my soup. It's 6:45. I should've gone home at 5:00.

He doesn't want you here, Billie! Why are you putting in this effort for someone who clearly doesn't appreciate it?

I finish my soup and wash all the dishes I've used. I leave them on the rack to dry, thinking I'll put them away in the morning.

Suddenly, I'm fighting tears. Of course I'm coming back in the morning, but this is the first time since getting this job that I really don't want to come in. Maybe it's just that I've been here eleven hours. *Or maybe it's because your employer is an ungrateful...* I let the thought trail off, feeling convicted.

I'm sorry, Lord. It's just that I'm really beginning to question if I'm supposed to be here! I can't take much more of his coldness toward me!

Suddenly, I remember that I'm not always thankful. I know that God has provided for me on many occasions, and I've neglected to stop and say thank you. What gives me the right to treat Merrick Anderson like he's so much worse than myself?

I sigh and make my way back to the living room. What I see nearly causes me to laugh. Mr. Anderson is holding the glass and straw, trying to get the last few drops from the bottom.

"Would you like more?" I ask, trying not to laugh.

He simply holds out his glass. I take it and walk back to the kitchen.

***

After I put the leftover soup away, I go upstairs to "close up" the office. I shut down Mr. Anderson's computer, make sure I have all my things, and turn off the lights. Then I go back downstairs to see if my boss needs anything before I head home.

"What time is my appointment?" he croaks out.

"7:00. First one of the day."

He nods.

"I'll see you tomorrow, sir."

He looks surprised.

"What?" I ask innocently. "You didn't think I was going to stay home just because you have a few germs, did you?" I cross my arms. "Uh-uh. You're not getting off that easy. I need the money."

I swear he almost smiles.

***

I walk into the office at 8:00 sharp. I decide I don't need to be early today, because Mr. Anderson most likely isn't back from the doctor's yet. I'm right.

I settle in to my new little routine. I hang my jacket on the back of my chair and put my purse and phone in my bottom desk drawer. Then I head downstairs to make the coffee. Even if Mr. Anderson isn't up for a cup, I am.

When I step into the kitchen, I nearly run into Mrs. Joy.

Chapter 6

"Good morning," I say. "And happy birthday!"

She beams. "Thank you, honey. Did you see my flowers?" She gestures to the counter by the sink. There's an incredible wildflower arrangement in a pink sparkly square box. Sticking out from the top is a tiny mylar balloon that says "Happy Birthday!"

"Oh, they're just gorgeous!" I walk closer to get a better look.

"As I was coming up the sidewalk, the man was here to deliver them to me." Mrs. Joy looks as if she's been handed the keys to a new vehicle.

I smile, and once again I'm glad I found the sticky note yesterday.

We chat for a few moments as I make the coffee. I'm just stirring in my cream when the front door opens, then closes. I go to meet my employer by the door.

"Well?" I demand.

"It's viral. She told me to rest." He scowls as he hangs his jacket on the coat rack.

Mrs. Joy and I exchange a look.

"I'll go make some hot tea and honey," she says.

I'm grateful she's back.

Mr. Anderson looks at me. "You can have the day off, if you want." He turns and heads down the hall to what I assume is his bedroom.

I meet Mrs. Joy in the kitchen again and explain to her that there's leftover soup in the fridge. "He may be up to having some, if he's hungry."

She opens the fridge and stares at the huge container. "You made him soup?" Her eyes go wide.

"Sure." I shrug, like it's no big deal. "You're welcome to it, too. There's plenty."

She shuts the fridge and gives me a funny look. "You made him soup," she repeats.

Um.

"Did I do something wrong?" I ask.

"Wrong? Oh, no, no, no." She waves her hand. "It's just that, well, it's been a while since someone's done something nice for Merrick without expecting something in return."

"Oh."

I decide right then that I'm not going to take the rest of the day off. I look up in the direction of the office and smile. I have work to do.

Chapter 7

It's been two days since I've seen my boss. I walk in early Thursday morning, and he's sitting at his desk.

"Good morning," I say, a bit surprised to see him back to work so soon. "How are you feeling?"

He nods. "Better."

"Good." I stand there, waiting.

Mr. Anderson goes back to his work. Without saying a word.

I sigh softly. I guess things are back to normal around here.

I was hoping he'd at least *comment* on the office. I know not to expect a thank you. But it'd be nice for him to just this once acknowledge what I've done.

I spent the last two days cleaning this office. I finished organizing—even taking on the dreaded task of his desk. Anything that looked remotely personal got put into his top drawer. I got some cleaning supplies from Mrs. Joy and scrubbed this place top to bottom. I even dusted every individual slat of the blinds covering the windows. This place looks *nothing* like it did the day of my interview. So much for acknowledgment for a job well done.

I walk over to my desk to start my day and I gasp softly when I see it. Gone is the square chair that's too low for my desk. In its place is a brand-new white leather desk chair. It's got chrome padded arms and a waterfall seat.

I run my hand over the back and smile. *It's so soft.*

I turn and look at the man responsible. He sits as if not a thing has happened. As if he was never sick.

As if I didn't take care of him. As if the office is still the same.

As if he didn't thank me by buying me a beautiful desk chair.

"Mr. Anderson."

He turns.

"Thank you."

He nods and goes back to his screen.

I sit down and try not to squeal with delight. This has totally made my day.

***

The phone rings continuously. This military ball thing he's planning is quite the event of the season. It's planned for mid-December, so Mr. Anderson has about two months to work his magic. And work magic he does.

There are catering companies falling over themselves to offer their services, promising to beat the competition's prices and one-up their menu. They all gush about what an honor it'd be to be hired by Mr. Anderson. *Eye roll.*

It's nearing noon and Mr. Anderson stands. "Set the phone to voicemail, Miss Sterling. We're going to lunch."

"Um, we are?"

"We are." He's already got his keys in his hand. He waits.

"Oh… okay," I say, and hit the *after-hours* button on the phone.

I grab my stuff and follow him out.

I wait to see which vehicle he gets into before getting in myself. It's the Mercedes.

After I buckle, I prepare myself for a silent trip. He surprises me, however, by simply saying, "Your soup was good."

I smile. "Thanks."

"*Really* good. Probably the best I've had."

I blink. *Who is this person driving Mr. Anderson's car?*

"Wow. Thank you. I'm glad you liked it."

Chapter 7

He nods.
Then silence.
I relax, because this time it's not awkward.

* * *

We're seated at a booth by the window. We're at Antonio's Fine Italian and just walking in made my mouth water. The food here is five-star. I rarely come because, well, it's expensive and lately my budget is more in the McDonald's range.

The young waiter hands us our menus and fills our water glasses. He points out the special, Shrimp Stuffed Cannelloni, and I manage to keep my eyes from widening at the price. $32.99. For *lunch*.

"We need a minute," Mr. Anderson says.

"No problem," our young waiter says with a slight bow. He leaves us alone.

I quickly decide on the soup and salad. The price isn't too bad, and I don't think I can eat a heavy pasta dish anyway. Sitting across from my employer to share a meal has my stomach in knots.

Mr. Anderson has obviously decided what he wants, because he sets the menu aside and folds his hands and looks at me.

"Miss Sterling, we need something different for this Marine Corps ball. I need some ideas."

He's asking for my help? My *opinion*? I don't know whether to feel flattered or terrified. What if my ideas are stupid? *Ugh. I'm such a child.*

"Different, how?" I ask.

"Well, for starters, it's a week and a half before Christmas. Everyone will expect a Christmas theme. I don't want to do that." He takes a sip of water.

"You don't?"

"No. I—"

The waiter reappears. "Are you ready to order?"

Mr. Anderson gestures for me to go first.

I order, then he does. When the waiter walks away, Mr. Anderson tries again.

"I want something different and unexpected. I'm not against having the season incorporated somehow, but I don't want the theme to simply be Christmas."

"Okay," I say thoughtfully. "I've never been to a military ball—any branch. Isn't there certain protocol for this type of thing?"

"Yes, but I'm not handling that. I'm hired to do theme, music, and food."

"Ah. Okay. Well, do you have any ideas so far? A starting point?"

He sips his water again. "No. Just that I don't want the same old thing. It's got to be spectacular."

Well, okay. Think "spectacular," Billie.

I open my mouth to throw out a few suggestions off the top of my head, and he holds up his hand.

"And don't even *think* about a prom-type theme. I don't want *Under the Stars* or *A Night to Remember*."

I close my mouth.

The waiter brings us a basket of bread sticks and I'm grateful for the interruption.

I wait to grab one, but Mr. Anderson digs in. I quickly bow my head in a silent prayer of thanks for our food.

When I look up and grab my own bread stick, my boss is staring at me.

"Why did you do that?"

"What? Pray over the food?"

"No. Pray over just your *own* food."

My face heats. "I… I just didn't think…" I don't really know what to say.

"There you go assuming again, Miss Sterling."

"Mr. Anderson, I'm sorry, that was rude of me."

"Apology accepted. Now, what are your thoughts on the ball?" He takes a huge bite of his bread.

Alright then.

"I'll have to give it some thought," I say. "Let me do a little research. If you think of something in the meantime, I'd be glad to share my thoughts."

Our food comes just then and we're both quiet as we start eating.

After a moment, Mr. Anderson says, "I'm expecting someone this

Chapter 7

afternoon. Prescott Wakefield. We'll be discussing a special tribute for a retiring sergeant major."

"Okay," I say, dipping a bread stick in my soup. "Will you need me for anything?"

He shakes his head. "Just send any calls for me to my voicemail."

I nod.

"And put on a fresh pot of coffee."

"Got it."

We continue eating and Mr. Anderson is silent again. I'm learning that he doesn't care for small talk. If there's no pressing matter, he doesn't say anything at all.

When the bill comes I reach for my purse, remembering our separate orders at the coffee shop. But to my surprise, my boss grabs the bill and takes out his wallet.

"Oh, thank you," I say softly.

"Of course," he says, and I'm sure I detect a bit of offense in his answer. He pays and leaves a generous tip.

And just like that, our lunch is over.

The ride back to the office is just as quiet as the meal.

* * *

Prescott Wakefield arrives just before 3:00. He looks to be about my age, and though he's not quite as tall as my employer, he's nearly six feet. And he's handsome. Very much so.

So, when Mr. Anderson introduces us, I blush like a schoolgirl when he shakes my hand and smiles warmly. He's got very short, neatly cropped blonde hair, and dark brown eyes. I learned earlier from Mr. Anderson that he's been in the Marines since he graduated high school ten years ago.

"Miss Sterling, it's nice to meet you."

"You as well," I say hoping my grin doesn't *look* as silly as it *feels*.

"Where did you find such a lovely assistant, Merrick?" he asks, his eyes lighting with humor. "If it was an agency, I'm gonna need that number. All the office workers at the base are ugly Marines." He winks at me before looking back to Mr. Anderson, whose face would be lethal if looks alone could kill.

I swallow hard. *He's got to lighten up! Can't he handle a little joking?*

"Would you like some coffee, Mr. Wakefield?"

"I would love a cup."

"Cream or sugar?"

"Just cream," he says with a devastating smile. "If you make it, it'll be sweet enough."

I laugh at his attempt at flirting. "I'll be right back. Mr. Anderson, would you like a cup?"

"No."

He looks angry. *God forbid I have a little fun at work.* I turn to head down to the kitchen. And when I close the door behind me, I roll my eyes.

* * *

When I return with Mr. Wakefield's coffee, he's already in deep conversation with Mr. Anderson. They've got papers spread in front of them and pencils in their hands, making notes. Suddenly, I feel a little sense of pride in the job I've done in organizing my boss's desk.

Trying not to interrupt, I quietly set the coffee beside Mr. Wakefield. As I turn to walk to my desk I hear, "Thank you."

I turn back and give him my warmest smile. *Someone* should take a cue from this guy. "You're very welcome," I say.

"As I was saying," my employer begins, a note of irritation in his voice, "here is a list for…"

I walk back to my desk as he goes on. When I sit down, I glance his way. Mr. Wakefield's back is to me, but Mr. Anderson is looking past him to me. When my eyes meet his, he turns back to the paper in front of him.

Weird.

I hear my phone buzz from inside the desk drawer, so I get it out and glance at it. It's my dad calling. I answer in case it's important.

Chapter 7

"Hey, Dad," I say quietly.

"I'm sorry to disturb you at work, Billie. But did you pick up my new prescription yesterday?"

I put a hand to my forehead. "Dad, I'm so sorry. I completely forgot."

"It's alright," he says. "I just wanted to make sure you didn't drop it off to me and I misplaced it."

"I'll get it on my way home."

"No worries. I'll let you get back to work."

"Okay, do you need me to grab anything else?"

"I think I'm good."

"Alright. See you soon."

We end the call and I put my phone back in the drawer.

Mr. Anderson is watching me.

Shoot. Is he upset that I answered my phone?

He stands and walks to my desk.

"Sir," I begin, "that was my dad—"

"Is everything alright?"

"Yes, but—"

"Your call sounded urgent. If you need to leave early today, it's alright."

Um.

I look at him, confused.

"I'll pay you for a full day, of course."

It would be nice to get home early and spend a little extra time with my dad. I haven't seen him all week.

"Alright," I say slowly. "I guess I'll see you tomorrow, then?"

He nods and walks back to his desk.

I gather my things and make my way to the door.

"Leaving so soon?"

I turn and look at Prescott Wakefield, who truly looks disappointed.

"Uh, yeah," I say, still confused at what just happened. "My dad needs me, so I'm taking off a little early."

He stands and holds his hand out to shake mine again. "Well, it was certainly a pleasure meeting you, Miss Sterling. I hope we'll see each other again."

I take his hand and smile. "Likewise," I say, and mentally chastise myself for sounding shy.

We're standing there, smiling at each other, when a cold voice says, "Goodbye, Miss Sterling."

Oh, right.

"See you tomorrow, sir."

I walk out of the office, puzzled. As weird as it sounds, I feel a little rejected. It's like my employer couldn't wait for me to leave.

Chapter 8

"I don't know, Anne," I say to my cousin that night over video chat.

"Come *on*, Billie. He's a really nice guy."

I sigh. "To be honest, I'm just not interested in being set up right now. With my dad's health, and my new job…" I shake my head.

"You still need to have a social life, Bill," she says, twirling a strand of her blonde hair.

"Yeah, I know that," I say, defensively. "It's just that… well… if I *was* going to start dating…"

Anne's eyes go wide and she gets too close to the screen. "You have someone in mind?"

"Well… I kind of met someone today." I grin.

"Billie Alexandra Sterling! That should have been the conversation starter!"

I laugh. "It's no big deal. It's not like he asked me out or anything. We just met, and… flirted."

"Start. At. The. Beginning," she says.

"Well, he's sort of a client of Mr. Anderson's. He came in today, and I immediately found him very attractive."

"Details!"

I have to turn my phone volume down for Anne's squealing.

"Well, he's a Marine," I start off by saying.

Anne nearly swoons. "Go on!"

"He's tall, and—"

"Nicely built??"

"Stop interrupting!" I laugh. "But yes, nicely built." I blush.

"Is he dark and handsome like Merrick?" she teases.

I ignore that. "He's blonde. And he's got these warm, deep brown eyes..."

She laughs. "Wow. It's been a long time since you've talked about a guy like this. What's his name?"

"Prescott."

"He sounds rich."

I laugh again. "You are so stereotypical."

"It just sounds like he should play tennis."

"You're crazy."

"We're related."

"Unfortunately," I tease. Then I sigh. "I just don't know when or if I'm going to see him again."

"Why don't you ask Merrick for his contact info?"

"That's an idea."

"So, tell me about this flirting you mentioned." She grins obnoxiously.

"Well, when we met, he asked Mr. Anderson where he found an assistant as *lovely* as me." I laugh. "So cheesy, right?"

"So *sweet!*"

I tell her about the coffee comment and about our goodbye. Anne thinks it's the beginning of an epic romance, and before we end the chat, she makes me promise to keep her posted.

"I'll try," I laugh.

After we say goodbye, I sit there for a while, thinking of the warm smile of a certain Marine.

* * *

It's mid-morning on Friday, and I've been wanting to ask Mr. Anderson about Prescott Wakefield. But the day has already been busy, and I haven't

Chapter 8

gotten the chance.

Finally, a few minutes go by without the phone ringing. Mr. Anderson is not on a call, and this seems to be the perfect opportunity. I stand and head over to his desk.

I lean on the side with my hand and go for it. "Excuse me, sir?"

His head never moves, but his eyes find mine.

"Um, I was wondering…" I don't know why I hesitate. "Would you happen to have Mr. Wakefield's phone number?"

He's quiet for a moment. Finally he says, "You know I do."

"Oh, okay, great. Um, can I have it?"

He stares at me.

Suddenly, a thought hits me. What if Prescott Wakefield doesn't *want* me to have his number? Blushing, I gush, "Oh my gosh, never mind. I shouldn't have asked."

I rush back to my desk and sit. *What was I thinking?*

The phone rings, and I pick it up quickly, thankful for the distraction. I answer a few questions for the gentleman on the other end and then hang up. As I do, I see a large hand in the corner of my vision.

Mr. Anderson sets a sticky note in front of me. It's a phone number, written in his bold handwriting. "Don't let it interfere with your job," he says coolly.

"Of course not," I answer.

I tuck the note in the front pocket of my purse and get right back to work.

* * *

After lunch, I'm in the kitchen making some fresh coffee and I run into Mrs. Joy.

"I've got to tell you," she says, "I'm sure glad Merrick finally hired someone." She shakes her head. "I've been getting more done around here than I ever have."

I laugh.

"It's the truth!" she goes on. "I used to be housekeeper *and* assistant. But I never got paid for both."

She scowls in her way, and I think back to how intimidated I was when she opened that door for the first time. I was sure she'd have me for breakfast. But now, I kind of find her rough-around-the-edges demeanor endearing. She's really a sweet lady.

"Well, you're not the only one who's thankful for him hiring me. I needed this job like you wouldn't believe." I pour the coffee grounds into the filter and turn on the pot.

"What's your story, anyway?" she asks, as she digs through one of the cupboards, looking for something.

"Well, it's always been just me and my dad. We've had it pretty great, until last fall. He got diagnosed with cancer."

"Oh my. I'm so sorry, honey. What kind?"

"Stomach," I say. "It's really taken him down. He can't work, and I'm supporting us both. He's got a ton of debt from losing his business years ago, and we just can't seem to catch up."

"Doesn't he get some kind of medical disability?"

"He does, but it's not enough to make ends meet." I shrug. "That's why this job is such a blessing."

The coffee is ready, and I pour two mugs.

"God has really taken care of us," I say. "When the owner of our apartments found out that I was basically my father's caregiver, he gave us a *great* deal on two apartments right next to each other. Now I can take care of my dad, and we each still have our privacy."

"Oh, that's wonderful," Mrs. Joy says.

"Well, I'd better get this upstairs," I say, holding up Mr. Anderson's mug.

"You'd better," she says, giving me a stern look. "He doesn't need to be put in a worse mood than he's already in. I swear, that man…" She trails off as she heads out of the kitchen.

What did I miss while I was at lunch?

* * *

Chapter 8

The afternoon flies by. Mr. Anderson is on the phone most of the time, and I've got a ton of paperwork to sort and file. We don't get to talk much.

Not that Mr. Anderson talks a lot, anyway. But there's always some kind of communication between his nodding and icy stares.

It's 5:07, and I'm setting the phone to *after-hours* when I notice he's not on a call anymore. I suddenly become bold and ask, "Any plans for the weekend, sir?"

He stops stacking the papers in front of him and looks at me. "I don't have time to *play*, Miss Sterling. There's work to be done."

"You work every weekend?"

"Most," he answers.

"That's too bad," I say.

"I enjoy my work. What's so bad about that?"

"Well, it's only bad when you enjoy your work and nothing else. Don't you ever spend time with friends or family?"

"That's none of your business, Miss Sterling."

I realize I've gotten too personal. "I didn't mean to overstep, sir. I'm sorry."

He says nothing.

I want to ask him something else, and I gather my things as I work up the courage. "Um, I actually was wondering…" I begin.

He's back to shuffling papers around his desk and I see him stiffen. "What is it?"

He doesn't seem like he really wants to answer any of my questions. But I ask anyway, because I really want to know.

"What kind of a guy is Mr. Wakefield?"

He does turn to me this time, his face void of any expression I can read. "Nice enough."

"Well, sir," I say as I walk to stand next to his desk. "I was kind of hoping for a little more than that."

"What do you wish to know?"

"I know he's a Marine, but other than that, I have no idea what he's like."

"That didn't seem to bother you when you were begging for his number." He turns to place something on the shelf behind him.

My face flames as I take offense to his comment. "You know what? Forget I asked. Have a nice weekend, Mr. Anderson." I turn to leave.

I'm almost to the door when I hear, "He believes like you."

I stop and turn. "What?"

"He's really into his faith. Goes to church and all that."

I stare at him for a moment, surprised that he knew that would be important to me. "Thanks," I say.

I turn back to the door and grab the knob. I look back and say softly, "Goodbye, sir."

He says nothing as I leave.

Chapter 9

"Dad. Tell me what Dr. Kimble said. You know I'll find out anyway." I'm in the small dining room, where I pull my dad's laundry from the little stacked dryer and stuff it in a laundry basket. I head over to the couch and begin folding.

My dad is sitting in the recliner across from me. He scrubs his hand over his face and looks at me. Finally, he says, "The treatment isn't working, Pumpkin."

I stop mid-fold and drop the towel in my lap. "What?"

"We knew the chances of this happening were high. They didn't catch it as early as we would've liked." He smiles sadly.

I stare at him, trying to process what he's said. All the fighting. All the prayers. "So, what do we do now?"

He sighs. "We make the most out of the time I have left."

"Dad," I whisper.

"What I *don't* want to do," he says, "is spend my last days being bitter and angry. I've trusted God this far. I know He'll be with me still."

I get up from where I'm seated and sit on the arm of his recliner. "How can you say that? How can you just accept this?" I feel the tears coming.

"I'm not at the point where I've *just* begun to accept this, Pumpkin." He puts his hand on mine. "It's been a long process, and I've had a lot of talks with God." He chuckles. "Or I should say, God has been very patient with me through the hours I've spent yelling at Him."

I laugh a little, but it's humorless.

My dad goes on. "About a month ago, Dr. Kimble gave me the name of a Christian counselor who deals with this sort of thing." He shrugs. "So, I gave him a call. Chuck has been taking me the last two Thursdays. It's been great to talk to someone."

I slide down the arm of the recliner until we're squeezed in the seat together. I lay my head on his shoulder. "Dad, I feel like *I* haven't been there to talk as much as you need. I'm sorry."

He pats my hand comfortingly. "You've done nothing wrong, Pumpkin. Nothing. If it weren't for you, I wouldn't have made it this far. You've worked so hard for me as well as yourself."

Suddenly I sit up and face him. I ask the question I'm dreading. "How long?"

He smiles. "I'll get to spend Christmas with you."

"Oh Daddy!" I throw my arms around him and sob. I'm hit with a tidal wave of emotions just then, and I let the tears come. He holds me and lets me cry.

* * *

I wake up and look at my clock. 10:20. I've slept in later than usual, but I needed it. Without looking in the mirror, I can feel that my eyes are swollen. I cried myself to sleep last night.

Feeling emotionally drained, I go to the kitchen to start my coffee. And I pray.

I let everything out in a long, emotional rant that barely resembles a prayer. I'm thankful that God doesn't have specifications or outlines to follow. Because what I pour out to Him now is an absolute mess.

I sit at the table for a while, just being quiet and letting my Heavenly Father comfort me in the way only He can. As devastating as my life is becoming, I know He'll be there every step of the way.

I finish my first cup of coffee and my tears have finally dried. I grab my

Chapter 9

purse and unzip the front pocket. I pull out the yellow sticky note with the number I asked for printed in neat handwriting. I stare at it for a long time, thinking.

Then suddenly I grab my phone. I don't want to waste time thinking anymore. I dial the number and wait.

It rings a few times, then my call gets sent to voicemail. I panic, because I haven't had time to rehearse what I'm going to say.

I hear the beep. "Um, hi, Prescott? I mean, Mr. Wakefield! I don't know if you remember me, but my name is Billie Sterling. We met in Mr. Anderson's office the other day. Well, I kind of asked for your number, and…" I run out of words. "Call me if you want to." I end the call.

I stand there for a few seconds, and then I burst into laughter.

"Oh. My. Gosh. What was *that*, Billie? You are so ridiculous!" I say out loud. I put my hand over my face and try to calm myself down.

Then my phone rings and I freeze.

I recognize the number I just dialed. I'm glad it's not a video chat because I can feel my face heating. I put on my best *I'm-totally-cool-and-not-a-dork-at-all* voice and answer.

"Hi, Billie," says a deep voice that's laced with amusement. "I apologize for sending you to voicemail. I do that with numbers I don't recognize."

"I do too," I blurt out. "I mean, hi! Hi, Mr. Wakefield. How are you?" I slap my forehead. *Get yourself together!*

A deep chuckle and then, "I'm doing very well, Billie. And please call me Prescott."

"Okay," I say.

"I'm glad you called."

"You are?" I ask.

"Very," he says. "I could've kicked myself for leaving Merrick's office that day without getting *your* number."

I begin to relax. So, he *is* interested…

"Cool," I say. *Ohmygosh. Cool?* I cringe at my own word.

He laughs. "Very," he says again. "There *is* an important reason I wanted to talk with you again, Billie."

"Oh?" I say. I don't trust myself to say much more.

"Yeah. I know we had just met, and I hope you don't mind, but after you left, I asked Merrick if you were single."

My pulse speeds up.

"And I asked for a very specific reason."

"What reason?" I ask, and to my horror, my voice is barely a squeak.

"Well, the reason would be that I don't want to take an attached lady to the ball."

I swallow hard. "The ball?"

"Yes. Billie, if you don't have any other plans, I would like to ask you to be my date to the military ball in December."

Before I can think about it, I answer. "I would love to go with you," I say, maybe a little too enthusiastically.

Prescott laughs again, and says, "I'm *so* glad you said yes. I'd be embarrassed to face you next time I'm in Merrick's office, had you said no."

Now it's my turn to laugh. "I'm a little surprised you're asking me though," I say. "We just met, and well…" I hesitate and blush. "There must be a ton of girls lining up to be the date of a Marine," I say lamely.

"You'd be surprised," he says, and I can hear the smile in his voice. "Besides, when you meet a beautiful girl you're interested in, you can't waste any time, or another guy might snatch her up."

I'm blushing furiously now, and I'm thankful he can't see me.

"Um, thank you," I say.

Prescott is great at making small talk, and we chat comfortably for the next few minutes.

Finally, he tells me that he's got a busy day ahead of him, so he'd better go.

"Oh, okay," I say. I'm slightly disappointed. I'm enjoying our conversation.

"But," he starts. "I don't want to hang up without you agreeing to go out with me, *before* the ball."

"Name the date and time," I say, smiling.

"Is tomorrow night too soon?"

"No, tomorrow night is great."

"Great. I'll call you tomorrow after I get home from church and we'll plan

Chapter 9

something."

"Okay," I say.

After we end the call, I smile for a *really* long time.

* * *

"Your turn."

Anne hands me the dice and I roll. We're in my dad's apartment, playing Monopoly. After I hung up with Prescott, I called her and filled her in on my dad. She insisted on coming and spending the evening with us.

"Eight," I say, and move my thimble.

"You owe me…" Anne picks up Ventnor Ave. "$22." She holds out her hand and smiles.

"Ugh!" I complain, feigning anger. I hand over the colored bills.

My dad laughs as he takes his turn.

"So…" I say, a little nervous to share my news. "I, uh, have a date tomorrow evening."

Anne squeals and Dad gives me a smile. A huge one.

"The Marine?" Anne practically shouts at me.

Laughing, I say, "Yes, the Marine."

My dad waits patiently for me to explain. I tell him about Prescott, our first meeting, and our phone conversation. The phone conversation is new to Anne, and while she's hanging on my every word, I swear she never even blinks.

"So, he goes to church? That's a plus!"

"For sure," I say. "And by our conversation yesterday, he seems to be serious about his faith."

My dad chimes in. "Am I going to get to meet this Marine before you go?" His eyes twinkle.

I lean over and kiss his cheek. "Of course, Dad. When we make our plans, I'll ask him to come by here first."

Dad is looking at me funny, with sort of a goofy smile.

"What?" I ask.

"I'm just… glad. Relieved. Excited." He shrugs.

"Relieved?"

He sighs. "You've spent a lot of time taking care of your old dad, Pumpkin."

"Dad…" I begin.

He holds up his hand, cutting me off. "I'm not implying it's a bad thing. I've cherished every minute."

I notice Anne quietly get up and take her cup to the kitchen, giving us a moment.

Dad continues. "You've given up more than you realize, taking care of me. I'm glad to see you planning something for *you*."

"Dad, this won't interfere with our—"

"Stop," he interrupts. "You don't know how much joy it brings me to hear you talking about going on a date." He grins. "And no matter how I feel, I'll still whip any guy that even *thinks* about mistreating you."

I reach over and hug my father fiercely. He's amazing and I tell him so.

The rest of the night is spent laughing and attempting to finish our game, which is impossible because we become so silly and ridiculous that we can't even keep track of whose turn it is. But we have fun. And this is an evening spent with my dad that I'm sure I'll remember forever.

Chapter 10

I'm home about twenty minutes and I'm making myself lunch when my phone buzzes in my pocket. I grab it and see that it's Prescott.

"Hello?" I say in my sweetest voice.

"Hey. How was church?"

"Great. Yours?"

"Same. What are you up to now?"

"Making some lunch."

"*Mmm.* Sounds good."

"You don't even know what I'm having!" I laugh.

"Well, what are you having?"

"I'm actually using my panini maker for the first time."

"Oh? Did you just get it?"

I pause, trying not to laugh. "I've had it for over three years."

Prescott laughs, and I love the sound. "What made you get it out and use it today?"

"Fall is officially here, and I guess that makes me want hot sandwiches. Plus, I thought a grilled chicken panini would go great with my pumpkin spice coffee."

He groans. "You're a *pumpkin spice* girl?" I hear the teasing in his voice.

"Yes. And proud of it."

He continues to harass me about my love for all things fall, and I give it right back to him. He's easy to talk to and joke with.

Finally, he says, "Actually, I'm really glad to hear that you're into fall."

I laugh. "I live in Michigan; I kind of have no choice."

"Well, I planned on taking you to the big corn maze everyone's been talking about. Then dinner afterward?"

I smile. "That sounds perfect."

"Great."

"Hey, Prescott," I say, a little unsure.

"Yeah?"

"Um, I know this is our first date, and it's a little soon to meet the parents, but I was hoping that you wouldn't mind stopping in and saying hello to my dad?" I hold my breath, waiting for his answer.

"I'd love to meet your dad, Billie."

I let out my breath. "Thanks."

"Is everything alright?"

I decide to tell him. "My dad is sick."

"Oh no," he says. "Do you want to make it another night? We can—"

"No, Prescott," I say, gently cutting him off. "It's cancer."

"Oh, geez. I'm sorry, Billie."

"Thanks," I say. "He just doesn't have much time left, because the treatments…" The words get stuck in my throat and I feel my eyes start to burn.

"Billie. It's okay. We can talk about it later. I'll stop by around 2:30–is that okay?"

I swallow to get my voice back. "Perfect," I say. I give him my address and we end the call.

I sit for a moment while my lunch cools. Am I really ready to start dating?

* * *

It's 3:45 and we're driving to the corn maze in Prescott's blue Silverado.

"That went really well," I say. "Dad likes you."

Prescott glances my way, then back to the road. He smiles. "You think so?"

Chapter 10

"Okay, Mr. Charming. Enough with the false modesty," I laugh. "He didn't want you to leave."

"Very true," he says, still smiling. Then suddenly he gets serious. "Your dad seems like a great man, Billie. He cares about you a lot."

"He's the greatest," I say softly. "And I know he does."

We're quiet for a few moments and I reflect on the last hour. From the moment we walked into my father's apartment to the moment we left, Dad treated Prescott like a hero. But that's how my dad treats every man or woman serving our country. So I knew that even before he got to know Prescott, he'd respect him.

But it only took twenty seconds for my dad to fall under the charming spell of Mr. Wakefield, and soon he was genuinely laughing and enjoying the visit. We sat in his living room for an hour before I finally suggested we head out to the corn maze. I hated to leave Dad, but this *was* my first date with Prescott.

I turn to look out the window as we pull into the lot. Prescott looks for a parking spot while I take in all the people. There are moms and dads with teens, moms with strollers, and groups of kids. There are a few couples.

Prescott finds a spot and before I know it, he's at my door, opening it for me. He holds out his hand and I take it, smiling. After he helps me out of the truck and closes my door, though, he doesn't drop my hand, and I don't mind. We walk to the admission booth to get our tickets.

"I've never been here," I say. "This place is great."

It's an autumn dream. Pumpkins and haystacks, cider and donuts, and dad flannels everywhere. I grin as I take it all in.

"Want to walk around a bit before we start the maze?" he asks.

"Sure," I say. "Oh, look!" I point to a tunnel slide where kids are flying out the bottom, sitting on burlap sacks. "How cute are they?"

Prescott laughs. "Let's get donuts and cider, and we'll check everything out."

A few moments later, I have a steaming donut rolled in cinnamon sugar, and a paper cup with apple cider. I let out a dramatic sigh. "Ahhhh, now *this* is what fall's all about."

He grins at me. "You're adorable."

I turn away, so he can't see my cheeks redden. I'm not used to all this attention from a guy, but I find myself enjoying it.

"Oh, a bonfire!" I head in that direction. There's a little fence around the fire for safety, but you can get close enough to feel its warmth. We sit on the little benches provided and relax for a few minutes, eating our donuts.

"How are you liking your job?" he asks suddenly.

I take a sip of my cider. "I like it," I say. "Mr. Anderson isn't the easiest person to work with, but I'm getting used to him." I laugh. "During my interview, I literally imagined him picking me up and throwing me out the window."

Prescott throws his head back, laughing. "Merrick is not so bad," he says. "Just keep the focus on business and don't ever try to joke with him. You'll be fine."

"Why?" I suddenly ask. "Why is he so... *serious*?"

"I don't know all the details—we're more work acquaintances than friends. I just know he doesn't trust a lot of people. It has something to do with an incident a few years ago."

I swallow the last bite of my donut and brush the sugar from my fingertips with my napkin. "Oh," I say. "That's too bad. He seems like he doesn't enjoy life very much." I clap my hand over my mouth. "I'm sorry, I shouldn't have said that."

"It's okay," Prescott chuckles. "You're right."

I shake my head. "It doesn't matter. He's my boss. I have no business saying things about his personal life."

Suddenly, Prescott stands, his donut polished off as well. He can see I'm feeling uncomfortable. He holds out his hand. "Well, then. Shall we?"

I stand and grab his hand, thankful that he can turn an awkward moment into a comfortable one with ease. "We shall," I answer.

We head to the corn maze to tackle the beast.

* * *

Chapter 10

It was a good night. I'm sitting on my couch after checking on and saying good night to my dad. I'm debating whether I should call Anne or make her suffer. I look at my phone again. She has texted me three times tonight.

Omg how's it going??

Call me when you're home, Bill!! I want details!!

And finally, *I will literally die if I don't hear from you tonight.*

I roll my eyes. Anne is something else. But no matter how obnoxious she can be, she always makes me smile. I glance at the clock. 9:22. I pull up her number and hit the button to video chat.

She answers with a towel on her head and I laugh. "Hello, gorgeous."

"Billie! I was going to strangle you if you didn't call tonight. I even set my phone by the shower so I wouldn't miss you!"

"Anne," I deadpan. "In all this worry over my social life, have you ever thought about getting one of your own?"

She ignores my question and bulldozes on. "Did he kiss you goodnight?" Her eyes are positively shining.

"No," I say. "He was a perfect gentleman the entire night. He even walked me to my dad's apartment so he could say goodnight to him."

Anne falls back on her bed and the camera's view of her shakes. After positioning herself in the center again, she says, "I can't believe I waited all night for nothing."

"We actually had a great time," I assure her. "The corn maze was fun. It took us forever to find our way out, but we had a blast going through it."

"Where'd he take you for dinner?"

"Little Mexico," I say. Anne knows it's my favorite.

"So, he asked you for suggestions?"

"Yup," I grin.

"Soooo..." Anne draws out.

I raise an eyebrow.

"Do you think this could get serious, you and the Marine?"

I sigh. "I really don't know."

Anne sits up again, looking at me intently. "What do you mean, you don't know? Don't you like him?"

"I do," I say honestly. "I actually *really* like him, but..."

"*Uh-oh...*"

"As a friend."

"Oh no."

"He's great," I say. "We have so much fun when we're together or on the phone. But I'm so comfortable with him, like I would be hanging out with you. There's no..."

"Spark? Chemistry? Explosives?"

"*Explosives?*" I laugh.

"Yeah, you know, when love turns your whole world upside down."

"Anne, you need to write romance novels," I say.

"How do you know I don't already?" she says slyly.

"Stop it!" I start giggling and can't stop. Anne is ridiculous.

"My first book is about a Marine. Who plays tennis."

I laugh harder.

We continue to act like children for the next five minutes, then I get serious.

"I just really like Prescott and hope we can stay friends. I don't want to hurt his feelings."

"Understandable," Anne says. "I'll be praying for you."

"Thanks," I say, and mean it.

Chapter 11

I'm early. It's 7:48 when I walk into the office. Mr. Anderson isn't at his desk yet. I hang my jacket on the back of my chair and make a mental note to check into getting a coat rack. Even though Mr. Anderson lives downstairs, he keeps his jacket with him in the office in case he needs to leave from here.

I grab my pumpkin spice creamer and head down to make coffee. I've been drinking my coffee here instead of making it twice every morning, so decided to bring my own creamer.

I get to the kitchen and Mrs. Joy is already there, pulling muffins out of the oven.

I smile at her. "Good morning! I thought I smelled something good."

"Cranberry and white chocolate," she says, wearing a proud grin. "My mother's recipe."

I close my eyes and breathe in through my nose. "It smells wonderful."

"Make sure you take one, then."

"Thank you, I sure will."

I open the fridge to place my bottle of creamer in the door and I see it. Pumpkin spice, the same brand I buy. I laugh. "Mrs. Joy, are you a pumpkin spice fan as well?"

"What's that, honey?" She looks at me inquiringly.

I point in the fridge, then hold up my identical bottle. "The creamer. Is it yours?"

"Oh heavens, no." She waves her hand as if dismissing the idea. "I'm a tea drinker. That's Merrick's. I buy it for him every fall."

"Oh," I say, placing my bottle next to his. "Funny."

"How so, Miss Sterling?"

"Just that most guys I know tease me about my pumpkin spice addiction," I say. "It's funny to find a man that likes it."

Mrs. Joy gives me a knowing look, then turns back to her muffins.

I get the coffee grounds out of the cupboard and start the pot. While I wait, I take a napkin from the holder and carefully pull a hot muffin from the tray Mrs. Joy has set by me.

"Here, try this," she says, handing me the butter dish and a knife. I split my muffin in two and spread a little pat of butter on one of the halves. It melts instantly. I blow on it gently before biting into it.

"This is incredible," I say, my mouth full of muffin. Then I cover my mouth. "Sorry," I giggle.

"No worries, Miss Sterling. I'll take that as the highest compliment." She winks at me before saying, "Don't forget to take one up to Merrick with his coffee."

I nod.

In just a few moments, I have both coffees made and I'm headed up the stairs.

* * *

After saying good morning to my boss—who does not reciprocate—I move to his desk to set his coffee and muffin beside him. I'm about to turn and walk back to my desk when I pause. Mr. Anderson smells nice. *Really* nice. I've never noticed before.

"Do you need something?"

I flinch at the coldness in his voice before moving away from his desk. "No, sir. Just noticing that your cologne smells nice."

"I'm not wearing cologne."

Chapter 11

"Oh," I shrug, walking back to my desk. "Then I guess it's just you that smells good."

He turns and looks at me, one eyebrow raised in amusement.

My face and neck flame. *Why did you say that out loud, Billie?* I sit at my desk and avoid his gaze. I pick up the phone to check the voicemail from the weekend. When I chance a look his way, he's already back to staring at his screen. I blow out a soft breath. I don't know why I let him make me so anxious. I wish I could be as comfortable with him as I am with Prescott.

I roll my eyes. *Yeah, right.* The two men could not be more different. I try to picture my boss making his way through the corn maze and I nearly burst into laughter. Where Prescott was making jokes around every corner and thoroughly enjoying himself, Mr. Anderson would have a scowl plastered to his face, looking for someone to blame for the unpleasant time he was having.

I mentally scold myself for my own thoughts. I should be working, not daydreaming about my boss being in situations that make him miserable. But I have a feeling that if he's doing anything but working—he's miserable. Smiling, I get back to my work.

I'm going through some papers when I realize I could use a paper tray at my desk. Before asking to purchase one, I decide to go look in the storage room. I walk past Mr. Anderson, still avoiding eye contact. I get to the storage room and step inside, letting the door close behind me.

I spot a pile of office supplies that I know I've looked through before, but at the time I didn't know I'd need a paper tray. If we have one I might've missed it. I'm walking toward the pile when a book on one of the bookshelves catches my eye. I pick it up. *The Christmas Truce of 1914.*

I stare at it for a moment, then suddenly walk out of the storage room with the book in my hand and paper tray forgotten.

***

"It's perfect, sir."

Mr. Anderson looks at the book but says nothing.

"You wanted a theme, and I believe the word you used was 'spectacular.'"

"So I did."

"Mr. Anderson, *this* would be spectacular. *The Christmas Truce of 1914.* It's perfect!" I shoot him a confident smile. "And the best part is, no one's using it for their prom theme."

"How, Miss Sterling, do you suggest we incorporate this theme into the ball?"

"I haven't thought that far yet," I say, crossing my arms and pacing in front of his desk. "But I *know* this is a great idea. Just give me some time."

"We'll go to lunch today and discuss what you've come up with."

"I can't be expected to come up with something in three hours!"

"Tomorrow, then."

I groan. "I'll do my best."

He nods. "Well, Miss Sterling. I look forward to hearing your ideas."

Oh boy. I've got a little over twenty-four hours to come up with a doozy of a plan…

* * *

"Did you return Palmer Catering's call?"

"I did," I answer. "He said they were firm on their prices."

"Cross them off the list."

"Done," I say. I black their name out with a Sharpie.

"What about Gregory's?"

"Phone tag," I joke.

He nods.

"I can look up a few more places to add to the list," I say, opening my desk drawer to use my phone internet. A thought suddenly crosses my mind. "Would you mind if I brought my laptop in and used it here?"

Mr. Anderson is quiet for a moment, then says, "I have an extra one. I didn't think of it before now." He stands and moves toward the door.

Hmm. Who just has an extra laptop lying around? It's probably an old, outdated one. I hope it doesn't fall apart like the chair he gave me that first day.

He's gone no more than five minutes when he comes back into the office with a dark red laptop. My eyes go wide when I see that it still has the plastic covering on it and the cord is still bundled and tied with a huge twist-tie. This laptop has never been used.

"You just happened to have an extra *brand-new* laptop?" I say, incredulously.

"I don't like red."

"Uh, then why'd you buy it?"

"I didn't. It was a gift."

"Oh."

Mr. Anderson leans over my desk and opens the laptop. He's very close and I can smell him again. The thought makes me inwardly groan, embarrassed at my earlier remark. He reaches around me to put the plug into the side of the computer and I think how weird it is, him being this close to me. But it has not the slightest effect on him. He's paying no attention to me as his brow is furrowed in concentration.

"You may have to let it charge a while," he says. He stands straight now, stepping away from me. "Then I'll connect you to Wi-Fi and all that."

"Okay," I say. "Thanks."

Usually this would be the time he'd nod and walk away. But he just stands there. "Have you given any more thought to your idea?"

There's something about the way he says it, it's almost as if… as if he's looking for an excuse to stay at my desk and talk to me.

"Um, not really," I say. "I've been pretty busy with calls today."

"Oh. Okay, then. We'll talk about it tomorrow."

He turns and goes back to his desk. But I catch him turn and look at me one more time before going back to his screen.

Um.

"Is there something on your mind, sir?" I can't help but ask.

He swivels in his chair to face me. "It's nothing important. Just trying to plan ahead."

Now he's piqued my interest. I go to his desk, leaning on the side with my hand, as has become my habit. "That's kind of what I'm here for. To help you plan."

"Yes, but, well…"

If I didn't know better, I'd say he's nervous.

"The thing is, I've been invited to attend the military ball as an extended courtesy and, well, I thought you could accompany me since we're working together." He adds quickly, "As my assistant, of course."

Oh, no.

"Um, I actually already have plans to attend the ball, sir."

He stares at me, and I know the moment that he realizes what I'm going to say next because he beats me to it. "Prescott asked you."

I nod.

"Fine," he says. He goes back to his work without another word.

I walk back to my desk slowly.

Oh. My. Gosh. My hard-as-nails boss was going to ask me to the ball.

Chapter 12

As the remainder of the afternoon crawls by, Mr. Anderson goes from comfortably silent to icily silent. Except when he's on the phone, of course. Then he's *charming* Merrick Anderson. But when the phone call ends, he's back to sucking the heat out of the room with his personality.

I wish I knew a bit more about him. *Ha*, I think. Trying to get to know him on a personal level seems about as easy as turning a teacup poodle into a junkyard dog.

Lord, I pray silently. *Help me get to know my boss. If there's anyone capable of this impossible task, it's You! Help me to understand him better and get to know where he's coming from. Help me be his friend.*

Suddenly, I remember the photo of my boss as a boy, standing in a church. *And Father*, I add, *if there's a still a spot in his heart for You, help me reach it.*

I glance at my employer as he sits at his desk, his face lacking even the tiniest bit of warmth or softness. I can't help but think of how handsome he'd look if he smiled. And not the obligatory smiles he gives his clients and business associates. I mean a true, warm, heartfelt smile. I sigh, wondering if I'll ever see one on his stony face.

I hear my phone buzz from the bottom drawer of my desk and I decide to peek at it in case it's my dad. I pull the drawer open and glance at the screen. It's Chuck. Weird. He never calls me. I wonder for a second if it's a pocket-dial, then decide to answer just to see.

"Hello?" I nearly whisper, unsure of how Mr. Anderson would feel about me answering my cell during work.

"Billie. It's Chuck."

"Hey Chuck." I start to ask if I can return his call later when he cuts me off.

"Your dad just got taken to the hospital by ambulance."

I stand up, knocking my pencil and a few papers onto the floor. "*What?*" I ask, no longer worried about the volume of my voice.

Chuck continues and I can tell he's fighting to keep his voice calm. "He passed out while we were eating lunch. I called 911 immediately. He's at St. Mary's."

"Omygosh, I'll be there as soon as I can." I end the call without saying goodbye.

My hand is shaking as I try to gather my things to leave. Suddenly I notice my boss standing next to me.

"What's wrong?" There is genuine concern in his dark eyes.

"M-my dad," I struggle to get out. "He got rushed to the hospital. I need to go." I'm trying to go through my purse for my keys, but my eyes are blurry from the threatening tears and I let out a small sob. I finally grasp my keys and pull them out.

I feel a warm hand cover mine and gently take the keys from my hand. "I'll take you," says a voice that sounds remarkably like Mr. Anderson's but can't be, because it doesn't feel anything like a cold dagger.

But it *is* his voice.

"Sir?" I say, swallowing.

"You're too upset to drive. You'll be a danger to yourself and others on the road. I'll take you," he repeats.

"Th-thank you," I say. I grab my jacket.

I feel the jacket slip from my hands as Mr. Anderson holds it up for me to step into. I slide my arms into the sleeves and turn to face him. He places both hands on my arms and looks at me, his eyes caring. "Are you okay?"

"I don't know," I admit.

"Let's go then. What hospital?"

Chapter 12

"St. Mary's."

Mr. Anderson nods, then reaches over me to turn the phone to *after-hours*. Then he takes my arm gently and leads me to the door.

* * *

We arrive at St. Mary's in less than twenty minutes. Mr. Anderson pulls up to the ER door and stops.

"Go on in," he says. "I'll be right behind you."

I jump out and nearly run through the doors. I find the information desk and rush to the lady sitting behind it.

"I'm here to see my dad—he was brought in not too long ago," I say. I know I sound panicky.

"Okay, honey. What's his name?"

"William Sterling."

She types quickly on her computer, and in a few seconds she has his information in front of her. "Down that hall," she points behind her, "and make a left at the end. Room 30."

"Thank you!" I say, and I start to run off. I suddenly stop and turn back to her. "Uh, a man will be coming in in just a minute. He's with me. Please tell him I went back."

"Sure thing."

I head back to my father's room, my heart pounding. It takes me no time at all to find it, and as I near the door I feel nauseous. I don't know what I'll find. My nerves are in control now and I grab the knob with a sweaty hand. I open the door slowly.

"Dad?" I choke back my worried tears and step inside.

A nurse is standing next to my father, hooking up an IV. She looks over at me and smiles.

A smile is good!

"You must be Billie?" she asks me.

"Yeah," I say. "What happened?"

"Your father is extremely dehydrated. It caused him to black out earlier.

But we're getting some fluids going right now."

I crumple into the chair next to my dad's hospital bed and put my hand to my forehead. "*Dad,*" I say, my voice strained, "you scared me half to death!" I can't stop the few tears that roll down my face. Tears from fear or relief, I don't know.

My dad reaches over and takes my hand. I can feel that his strength is gone. "I'm so sorry, Pumpkin. I'm so sorry to scare you."

I bring his hand to my lips and plant a kiss on the back of it. "I *told* you that I didn't think you were drinking enough water!"

"I know and I should've listened. You take better care of me than I do." He smiles and points the plump, middle-aged brunette by his side. "This is my nurse, Julie."

"Hi," I say. "Sorry for the freak-out."

"Understandable," she says. "It's very nice to meet you. William has mentioned you several times."

I glance at my dad and smile; he shrugs.

"Oh!" I say, suddenly remembering Mr. Anderson. "Um, my boss drove me here—I should probably go out there and tell him what's going on. I'll be right back."

"Why don't you bring him in," my father suggests.

"Are you sure?" I give my dad an apprehensive look.

"I'm more than sure. Bring him on back."

I nod and step out into the hallway. I walk slowly back to the waiting room.

As soon as he sees me, Mr. Anderson stands. I can see the concern in his eyes from across the room. He steps toward me as I near him.

"Well?" he demands.

"He's dehydrated," I say. "It caused him to black out. He's on an IV now. He's very weak, though."

Mr. Anderson lets out a relieved sigh and I'm more than a little surprised at how it touches me. He genuinely seems to care about my father, whom he hasn't even met. Oh. Speaking of...

"Would... would you like to come back and see him?" Then I quickly add,

Chapter 12

"You don't have to if—"

"Yes."

"Um, okay. Follow me, then." I lead him back to my father's room and suddenly feel nervous. Much more nervous than when my dad was about to meet Prescott.

We get to the door and I push it open and step inside. My boss follows me.

"Well," my dad says, his voice still a bit weak. "Who do we have here?"

I blush at the tone of his comment. He says it as if I'm in middle school and introducing him to a boy.

"Dad," I say, "this is Mr. Anderson, my boss. Mr. Anderson, meet my dad, William."

Mr. Anderson warmly shakes my father's hand and tells him how nice it is to meet him. Then he asks him to call him Merrick.

"Merrick," my dad says, as if testing the name out on his tongue. "I like it."

"It was my grandfather's name," Mr. Anderson says. Then he turns to me. "And it seems I'm not the only one who's named after someone."

"Yeah," I say, chuckling. "If I had been a boy, I'd be William as well." I shrug. "But they still made it work for a girl."

His eyes find hold mine for a second. "I like it," he says, using my father's words.

Um.

"I'm sorry you both left work for me," My father says.

My gaze goes to him, but Mr. Anderson is the one to speak.

"It's not a problem, William. Getting your daughter here was priority. Had she just run out like she tried to do, I would've wondered all this time if she'd made it here. She was in quite a panic."

"That's my Pumpkin," Dad says, and I blush.

Oh Lord, Dad.

Mr. Anderson glances my way but doesn't smile. I'm sure he's just letting me know he noticed the use of my nickname.

"Can we get you anything while we're here?" I ask, needing something to do.

"I'd love some juice." My dad rubs his throat. "I've got this IV but I'm just so thirsty."

"Of course," I say, turning to the door. "I'll be back in a few."

"I'll go with you," a deep voice says from behind.

I step out of the room and my boss does, too.

We're following the signs to the cafeteria when he asks me, "Are you alright?"

"Of course."

"You seem a little shaken."

"Wouldn't you be, if your father who's dying of cancer gets rushed to the hospital?" I don't mean to sound as irritated as I do.

Mr. Anderson stops, halting me as well with a gentle pull of my arm. He turns me to face him. "Your father is dying?" he asks.

Oh. Right. We've never talked about this. "Yes," I whisper.

He looks at me seriously, but the usual coldness that accompanies his stare isn't there. "I'm sorry."

"Thank you."

I turn to start walking again but he grabs my arm. I turn back to him.

"If you need *anything*..."

I give him a half smile before saying, "Thanks. I'll be sure to let you know."

As we continue walking to the cafeteria, I decide that I can *definitely* get used to this side of Merrick Anderson.

Chapter 13

I was at the hospital pretty late last night. Around 5:30 Mr. Anderson drove us back to his house, where I jumped into my own car and headed back to the hospital—but not before Mrs. Joy handed me a cooler bag packed with containers of food. She insisted that I didn't need to eat that hospital food when she had made chicken and dumplings. I took it gratefully. I was at the hospital until 1:00 am.

So this morning I wasn't surprised when I got a text from my boss, that simply said, *Don't come in today. Stay with your dad.* I didn't have the mental or physical energy to argue, so I simply texted back, *Okay,* and headed up to the hospital.

Now it's after lunch and I watch my dad sleep. He seems so exhausted. Not that he had much energy before, but now he looks completely drained.

My phone buzzes in my pocket. I pull it out and see a text from Prescott.

Hey! Sorry I haven't called. Been working. How's it going?

I decide to forgo the small talk and get to the point.

Dad's in the hospital. Been here since yesterday. Dehydration. He's doing okay, now, though.

Oh, man. I'm sorry, Billie. What hospital?

Thank you. St. Mary's.

Can I do anything?

No, but I appreciate the offer.

No problem. I'll let you get back to your dad.
Thanks, Prescott.
Anytime.

I put my phone back in my pocket, comforted a little. Prescott's friendship means a lot to me. I should've let him know yesterday what was going on. I could've used the support.

You had support, Billie.

I think of my boss. It was nice seeing a softer side to him. It makes me wonder what he hides beneath that cold exterior. I remember that Prescott told me there had been an incident. What kind of incident causes you to shut out everyone around you with your iciness?

My thoughts are interrupted as my dad wakes. I reach over and place my hand on his, letting him know I'm here. He turns to me sleepily.

"Hey, Pumpkin."

"Hi, Daddy," I say softly. "How are you feeling?"

"Tired."

I nod. "I can imagine."

He smiles at me. "Where's Merrick?"

"In his office, I suppose."

"I like him."

I laugh. "That's because he was nice to you."

His eyebrow lifts. "He's mean to *you*?"

I puff my breath out. "Not exactly mean. He's just… not nice."

Dad smiles. "Give him time."

"To be honest, Dad, he kind of surprised me yesterday. From the time I got Chuck's phone call, to the time he left here, he was so supportive." I shake my head. "He was like a totally different person."

"It sounds like when it comes to the important things, he lets his guard down a little."

"Is that what you think it is? He has his guard up with me?"

"You've heard the rumors as well as I have, Billie. People don't speak well of his character. They eat it up when he makes a decision they can blow up into a good story. No one ever gives him the benefit of the doubt or stops to

Chapter 13

get the reasoning behind those decisions." He stops for a sip of his ice water, then continues. "Having his guard up makes him feel protected."

I smile at my dad's wisdom. "Thanks, Dad. That does help me understand him a little better."

Changing the subject to a lighter topic, I sit with my dad and chat until it's time to get dinner.

* * *

We're just finishing the potato soup from the cafeteria when nurse Julie walks in. "Looks like you'll be going home in the morning, William," she says with her bright smile.

Dad leans his head back on the pillow. "Thank the Lord."

I laugh. "But won't you miss the awesome food?"

He rolls his eyes. "Please. I can't wait for *your* cooking."

"Whatever you want tomorrow, I'll make it," I say.

Julie chuckles as she takes Dad's blood pressure. "Quite a daughter you have there, William." She winks at me.

"He takes me for granted," I say, teasing.

"Well, get used to it, honey. *All* men take us for granted," Julie says.

"Hey now, I'm outnumbered, here," my dad says, good naturedly.

"Not anymore," says a familiar deep voice.

"Prescott!" I say, surprised to see him standing in the doorway. I stand to hug him. "Thank you for coming."

"Of course," he says, and hugs me tightly back. "I just had to wait until after my shift."

"How are you, Prescott?" my dad asks.

"How am *I*? How are *you*?"

Dad laughs. "I've been better."

Nurse Julie gathers her things and makes her way to the door. When she passes by me, she nods her head toward Prescott and gives me a thumbs up.

I cover my mouth to suppress my laughter and shake my head. *Just a friend*, I mouth.

She gives me the *sure, he is* look, and exits the room.

"I appreciate you coming to see me, Prescott," my dad is saying.

"It's no problem," Prescott says. He sits in a chair near the foot of my dad's bed.

We chat for a few minutes, then I excuse myself to take a walk to the cafeteria. I've been sitting most of the day and need to stretch my legs. Prescott offers to go with me.

I give him a complete update on my dad as we walk through the hallways. "So," I finish, "you can see why everything with my dad is just a little more serious. More complicated."

"Yeah," he says, shaking his head. "Wow. Your poor dad."

"He really goes through it," I say sadly.

We get to the cafeteria and I order a decaf coffee. We find a small table off to the side and sit. As I stir in my cream, Prescott reaches over and gently lays a hand on my arm.

"Billie, I want to come by this Saturday and make dinner for you and your dad."

"Oh, you cook?" I ask.

He leans back, placing both hands behind his head as if he's lounging, and grins. "Very well."

I laugh. "We'd love to sample your cooking."

"Great. I'll come around 3:00. That will give me time to prepare."

"Prepare?" I raise an eyebrow. "Will this be a fancy dinner?"

It's his turn to laugh. "Hardly. I really only make two things, and neither is fancy."

"Which of the two will we have the pleasure of sampling?" I ask through my grin.

"Ah, now that's going to be my secret until Saturday." He suddenly gets serious. "Wait, do either of you have food allergies?"

"*Oh, no,*" I say, feigning fear.

"No, no, don't be afraid," he laughs. "That came out wrong."

"In all seriousness," I say, "My dad does lose his appetite quickly. And sometimes he doesn't want to eat all day."

Chapter 13

"There will be no offense taken if that happens," he says.

"Thank you," I say, smiling. "I appreciate the gesture."

"Of course," he says. "It's the least I can do."

I finish my coffee and we head back upstairs. My dad is asleep.

"I need to head home anyway," Prescott says quietly. "Please tell your dad I said goodbye."

"I will." I reach up and hug him again. "Thank you. So much."

He holds on to me for a moment. "Call me if you need anything."

"I will," I say again. He lets me go.

"Good night, Billie."

And then he's gone.

* * *

When I open the office door, Mr. Anderson seems surprised to see me.

"Miss Sterling. I didn't think you'd be in today."

"My father is doing much better," I say. "Our neighbor and good friend is bringing him home this morning. I figure he'll sleep most of the day, so why miss another day of work?"

Mr. Anderson nods. "I assume you'll need an extra day or two to come up with something for our Christmas Truce theme."

"Yes, sir," I say apologetically. "It hasn't exactly been in the forefront of my mind."

"Understandable."

I walk to my desk and put my things away. Hanging my jacket on the back of the chair reminds me of the coat rack. "Sir, I really feel we need a coat rack. Winter is coming, and we're going to have to hang more than a light jacket over our chairs."

"If this is something you wouldn't mind picking up, Miss Sterling, just hand in the receipt and I'll reimburse you."

That was easy.

"Okay, I don't mind at all," I say before heading to the door.

"Coffee's already on."

I turn to my employer. "It is?"

"I didn't expect you in today," he reminds me.

"Right." I say. "Well, I don't mind making us a cup."

He nods.

I walk down to the kitchen with what I know is an odd expression on my face. That is the most Merrick Anderson has spoken to me at such an early hour. Usually I tell him good morning and I'm lucky if I get a nod from him. I feel like he needs to warm up his vocal cords with a few phone calls before he really speaks to me.

A few seconds later, I'm pleased to run into Mrs. Joy in the kitchen.

"Ah, our meeting place," I tease, as she rushes to me.

"Oh Billie! I've been so worried about your dad. How is he?" Her brow is furrowed, face concerned.

"Thank you, Mrs. Joy," I say, hugging her. "That means a lot to me that you would ask." I fill her in on all the details.

I begin making two cups of coffee as I talk. "And your chicken and dumplings was amazing, by the way."

"Oh, thank you, but never mind that now." She waves her hand dismissively. "I didn't realize you hadn't told Mr. Anderson that your father has cancer, Billie. He told me everything, but I didn't tell him I already knew."

I shrug. "I guess I assumed he already knew somehow. It's not exactly a secret."

"Billie," Mrs. Joy begins.

"What?" I ask.

"I just want you to know… well, I thought I'd tell you, that Merrick doesn't do that sort of thing."

I cock my head to the side. "What sort of thing?"

"How he drove you to the hospital, and… stayed."

"Oh."

"Merrick has lived in his own bubble for a while now. It's nice to see him opening up a bit. Just…" She hesitates, choosing her words carefully. "Just be patient with him," she finally says.

"I will," I say softly. I don't know how, but in some strange way, I

Chapter 13

understand exactly what she's trying to say.

Chapter 14

It's Friday. The week is almost over and I'm thankful. My dad is back to his normal self—well, his new normal since dealing with cancer. I'm staying on him about drinking his fluids and I have Chuck checking in on him constantly.

"We're going to lunch today, Miss Sterling. I hope you've got your ideas together."

My stomach does a little flip at the thought of presenting what I've got to Mr. Anderson, but I nod. "Yeah. I'm ready."

I set the phones, grab my stuff, and follow him out.

While we're walking, I ask, "So, where are we going?"

"I was thinking Mexican Fiesta."

I love Mexican food, so I'm happy. "Sounds great."

I follow him to his Mercedes and climb in the passenger seat. He starts the engine and without thinking, I reach over and flip the radio on. It's set to the news.

Suddenly I remember it's not my car. I apologize.

"Don't be sorry," he says. "Go ahead."

The only station I really listen to is K-Love, so I find it and sit back in my seat. Mr. Anderson doesn't object, so I leave it on.

The current song ends and it goes right into a call from a listener.

"This is K-Love, what's your story to make us smile?" the male host asks.

Chapter 14

"Hi, my name is David," the caller begins. "*I just want to share that I've finally come home. My wife and kids have been praying for me for over three years...*" He pauses and you can feel the emotion through the radio. "*I guess you could call me the prodigal son. But two weeks ago, I finally decided I'd had enough. I went to church with my family, and I'm happy to say, I've rededicated my life to—*"

The caller is cut off when Mr. Anderson's hand hits the button, turning the radio off.

I look at him as he continues to stare at the road ahead.

I can't think of a thing to say, so I sit in silence until my boss speaks a few moments later.

"Great," he says. "They're closed."

We pull into the parking lot to see a few city trucks and workers. There's a sign on the front door of the restaurant, written large enough that we can see it from the car.

CLOSED DUE TO WATER MAIN BREAK.

Mr. Anderson loops around to head back the way we came.

I take a chance. "If you're in the mood for Mexican, sir, I can recommend another place."

He looks at me, waiting for my suggestion. I think.

"Uh, it's Little Mexico. It's about two miles east of here."

"I know where it is," he says. "But I've never been there."

"It's my favorite," I say. "The owner's mother is eighty-two years old and she's the cutest thing you've ever seen. She pushes a cart around with fresh avocados and makes guacamole right in front of you."

He nods and drives in that direction.

I smile. I'm glad we're going somewhere I feel comfortable—it takes the edge off my nervousness about sharing my ideas.

We arrive just a few minutes later in a silent car. I didn't even attempt to flip the radio back on. But in a weird way, I'm comfortable in the silence. Maybe I'm getting used to my boss's quiet nature. Who knows?

My thoughts are interrupted when I hear Mr. Anderson's door close. He bends slightly, looking at me through his window, his expression saying, *you coming?*

I jump out of the car quickly, making sure I grab the folder and the book I brought along. I pull my purse over my shoulder and turn to my boss. I smile. "Let's go."

* * *

Mr. Anderson loves the guacamole. Oh, he doesn't say anything—but he's eaten nearly the entire bowl himself.

I can't stop myself from saying, "I guess I'm going to have to call Mrs. Hernandez back over so she can flirt with you some more."

He scowls at me.

I laugh. "I could tell that she was fighting the urge to pinch your cheeks."

"I've had enough guacamole," he says, pushing the bowl away.

I try not to smile but I just can't help it. A grin spreads across my face. "Do you want me to get her number for you?"

Mr. Anderson is saved from further embarrassment when the waiter comes to take our order. I order the chunky beef burritos and he tells the waiter he'll have the same.

I raise an eyebrow in question after the waiter leaves.

"I figured that if this is your favorite place, you'd know what's good here."

"Very true," I say, pretending to have an air of pride. "See, you're smart. Prescott wouldn't take my advice and got stuck eating the fish tacos. Not that they're *bad*," I shrug. "They're just not the best thing on the menu."

Mr. Anderson stares at me and I'm surprised at the iciness that wasn't there a minute ago. "Prescott?"

"Yeah," I say carefully, wondering if I should tell him about our date. *He probably thinks it will interfere with work.* I decide to tell him anyway. "We went out last weekend."

He takes a sip of his Coke. "I see."

I feel the need to explain. "My seeing him won't interfere with work, sir. I promise."

Chapter 14

"Speaking of work," he says, "let's see your ideas."

I grab my folder and the book and set it in front of me. "Well," I begin, opening the book to a page I've marked. "For starters, it says here that they exchanged gifts such as tobacco and plum pudding. We could have a table set up among the refreshments with bowls of plum pudding to eat and little trays of tobacco—just for looks. We could label it 'Christmas Truce Gift Exchange.'"

I wait for him to respond.

He just says, "Go on."

Just then, the waiter comes with our food and I wait until we're situated to continue.

"Do you mind if I pray?" I ask.

He says nothing, but gestures to me to go ahead.

I give a simple prayer of thanks for the food and when I lift my head, I see that Mr. Anderson is watching me. I feel myself blush.

Still, he says nothing. I decide to go on explaining my idea.

"Then there are the carols they sang to one another. And before you think I'm crazy—hear me out. There is an outstanding boys' choir from St. Andrew's. They're known to do Christmas carols in a few different languages. I was thinking we could invite them to come and sing a few carols in German and a few in English. It will be like that night in 1914. Especially," I add with a clever look, "if we ask them to dress in apparel from the early 1900s."

Mr. Anderson just eats and listens, so I go on. "There are many photos online depicting what people think happened, drawings, or scenes from the movies that have been made. Either way, we could have life-sized cutouts of the opposing sides coming together in these exchanges. We'd keep the photos black and white, of course, for nostalgia purposes. It's even said that they played football together. We could have cutouts of that as well."

I take a deep breath and hold it for a second before digging into my plate of burritos. *This is it*, I think. *He's going to love it or hate it.*

My employer finishes chewing and swallows. "It'll do," he says, then takes another bite.

I smile and take my first bite.

He so likes it.

"Will this theme affect the dress in any way?"

"It's not a costume ball," I tease.

He doesn't appreciate my sense of humor. "I just didn't know if you had a specific theme for dress in mind."

"Well, the men would still wear their dress uniforms. But we could toss around the possibility of the women wearing dresses inspired by the fashion of that era."

He nods and chews.

"I just think it'll be a memorable way to remind everyone what this is all really about," I say between bites. "That a special occasion like Christmas is worth putting our differences aside and celebrating together."

I take another bite of food and chew for a moment. When I look up, Mr. Anderson is very still, watching me.

"What?" I ask, a bit self-conscious. *Do I have food on my face?*

"It's nothing. I just appreciate the way you think."

"Oh," I say. It's a huge thing, coming from the man sitting across from me. He doesn't seem the type to throw compliments around casually.

"Miss Sterling, I know tomorrow is Saturday, but would you be willing to take a ride with me? I'd pay you overtime, of course. We could visit some libraries and see what they have on the Christmas Truce. I know there are tons of things online, but it would be nice to physically go through some books and see pictures."

"I wouldn't mind at all," I say, more than a little excited.

He nods. "No need to get up early. Meet me at the office at ten?"

"Okay,"

For the next half hour, we bounce ideas off each other while we finish our meal. I'm surprised at how comfortable I'm beginning to feel around him.

* * *

The ride back to the office is a pretty quiet one. I may be getting more

Chapter 14

comfortable with him, but I certainly wouldn't classify us as *friends*. Sure, he's getting easier to talk to when it comes to work. But for the most part, he's still cold and distant—*especially* when it comes to anything remotely personal.

We walk into the office and I decide to keep my jacket on. It's as cold as ever in here. I set my phone and purse on my desk and ask my boss if he wants a cup of coffee. He says yes and I'm glad; I want one myself.

I'm back upstairs in no time, and when I walk inside, Mr. Anderson is bending over my desk, looking at my laptop and jotting something down on a sticky note. I set his coffee down and turn to my desk, waiting for him to finish.

I hear my phone buzz on the desk and it catches Mr. Anderson's attention. He glances at it then looks away. Then he stands and walks to his own desk, sticky note in hand.

"I just needed a number from a website you already had pulled up." He sits down and picks up his office phone and starts dialing.

I get to my desk and glance at my phone. On the lit-up screen is a text from Prescott.

It's been a long week. Can't wait to see you tomorrow.

Shoot. He's supposed to come over and cook dinner for me and Dad. I completely forgot. I suppose I can make it work if I leave for home by 2:30. Maybe Mr. Anderson will be willing to meet a little earlier.

I look in his direction and hear he's leaving a voicemail for someone. Then he hangs up.

Without turning to look at me he says, "Do we need to cancel tomorrow's outing, Miss Sterling?"

"No," I say quickly. Part of me would be disappointed if we do. "I don't have plans until three. We could even meet earlier than ten if you'd like," I say hopefully.

"Ten is fine." He's still looking at his screen.

"Okay," I say. I hope he's a little warmer with me tomorrow.

Getting back to my work, I sigh. So much for a relaxing weekend.

Chapter 15

I pull the long noodles out of the colander and plop them on my dad's plate. He loves spaghetti and I'm hoping his appetite is back tonight. I spoon the sauce and meatballs over the top and grab a small piece of garlic bread. I'm making my way to his recliner as he finishes opening his TV tray.

"It smells good," he says.

I smile. "Good. I hope you'll be able to eat at least half of this. Do you need a fresh water bottle?"

"I'm good." He holds up the one he's got.

I nod and return to the kitchen to make my own plate.

Finally, I situate myself on the couch with my food in my lap and ask my dad to pray. He does and we start to eat. Well, *I* start to eat. My dad begins pushing his food around his plate. I don't make a big deal out of it, though.

"So," I begin, "Are you excited about Prescott coming to make us dinner tomorrow evening?"

"I am," he answers, smiling. "I really like that guy."

"Me too."

My dad raises his eyebrows in question and I shake my head.

"Not like that," I say. "Well, at least I don't think so."

"Oh?"

"It's weird. I'm so comfortable around him—like we've been friends for years, even though I've known him such a short time." I pause to take a bite, chewing slowly. Finally, I swallow. "I just don't know if my feelings are romantic."

"I see," my dad says, nibbling his bread. "Do you have romantic feelings for anyone else?"

I stop chewing and look at him. "Um, no?"

He laughs. "You're unsure?"

"No, I just... who else would I...?" I blush.

"So, you're saying there's nothing between you and that boss of yours?"

"Dad!" I laugh, then point to his plate. "Eat your food."

"I'm not blind, you know."

I look at him.

"He's attracted to you."

"Dad. There's absolutely no way. He's as cold as a codfish. I think I'd know if he was interested in me. Besides, it doesn't matter. I'm not interested in him." I stuff my mouth with noodles so I don't have to talk anymore.

I see my dad shake his head and smile, but he doesn't say anything else.

Mr. Anderson is most definitely not attracted to me. And I am not... My thoughts trail off. I may be a *little* attracted to him. I've gotten used to the fact that his face looks like it's been chiseled from granite and will crack if he smiles. I've gotten comfortable sitting in cold silence while we work. I've learned to wear a sweater while at my desk and, well, it doesn't seem so chilly in there anymore. I've even caught myself staring at him for no particular—

Billie Alexandra! I mentally scold myself. *You cannot entertain these kinds of thoughts about your boss!*

The question is... why do I *want* to?

* * *

It's Saturday morning. I'm both looking forward to and dreading this day.

After dressing in jeans, an oversized brown sweater, and my favorite fall boots, I throw my hair in a casual ponytail and grab my jacket. I'm out the door sooner than expected, so I decide to stop at Sam's and get a coffee. When I get there, I order one for Mr. Anderson, too. If he doesn't want it, oh well. I don't want to show up with one for myself and not him. I add a few muffins to my order—I try to remember the ones he liked—then I head back to my car.

It's still a few minutes before ten when I pull up to Mr. Anderson's. I sit in my car and pray that today goes well. I pray once again that God would help me reach that spot in his heart that's still open to Him.

I get out of my car and knock on the big brown door that was once so intimidating to me. But this time, I'm not nervous at all about what's on the other side.

I half expect Mrs. Joy to answer the door and I'm surprised when Mr. Anderson does. Then I remember that it's Saturday and she's off.

"Hi." I hold out the coffee. "I got this, just in case you hadn't had yours yet."

He nods and takes the cup. "I haven't." He opens the door wide for me to step inside.

He doesn't thank me for the coffee, but I don't expect him to. Besides, I need a reason to roll my eyes as I step into the cold foyer.

"Just give me a minute and we can go," he says.

I notice he's very casually dressed, which I'm not used to seeing. He's got on dark jeans and a navy blue and white baseball t-shirt. He looks comfortable and… nice.

I watch as he slips on his shoes and grabs his jacket and keys, then I follow him out the door.

It's one of those perfect October days, where the leaves are turning and there's just enough of them scattered on the ground to make it feel like fall. The weather is chilly but not cold, and a warm coffee and a good sweater is all you need to feel cozy.

We reach the garage and I head to the Mercedes when Mr. Anderson stops me. "We're taking this today, Miss Sterling." He points to the black SUV.

"Oh, okay." I move to the other vehicle and climb inside.

As he's pulling away I say, "It's Saturday and we're taking a trip to the

Chapter 15

library. You can call me Billie if you want."

I wait for him to offer me the same courtesy, but he says nothing.

Okay, then.

Thankfully, it's only a five-minute drive to the library. We enter and quickly find a small table in one of the corners, where we can talk and not be disruptive. We sit down and I pull a small notebook and pen from my purse. "Well, let's get to it," I say quietly. "Where should we begin?"

* * *

It's after noon and we've found some pretty great books on the Christmas Truce. I'm starting to see why Mr. Anderson is so good at his job. The ideas he comes up with are unbelievable, and I'm excited to see the final results of his planning.

Suddenly, I remember I'm going to be there to enjoy the fruits of our labor. With Prescott. Why do I feel slightly disappointed? I'm excited to attend with him. I am... right? I shake my head. I can't think about this now.

I point to my notebook. "I hope I didn't forget anything."

The next thing I know, I smell pumpkin spice coffee as my boss leans over me to look at my notebook.

"It looks fine, Miss Sterling."

Yes. You do.

My face flames as my own thoughts surprise me. *Get a grip, Sterling! What's the matter with you?*

"Um, okay," I say, gathering my stuff. "We've probably got enough to work with for now." I drop my pen and it goes rolling under the table. I'm so flustered by this point that I bend to pick up, then stand up too quickly.

Crack!

Pain explodes in my head as I hit the corner of the table. "Oh, geez!" I rub the top of my head.

I feel strong hands grip my arms securely and gently sit me down.

"Are you alright?"

I look up. He's close. *Very* close.

"I… I'm okay," I say, staring into his brown eyes. The usual coldness isn't there. I smile. Then I close my eyes. I feel dizzy.

"Oh Lord, you're bleeding."

I must've hit my head harder than I thought. I reach up and touch the tender spot and when I pull my hand away, there's blood on my fingers.

"Come on," my boss says, helping me stand. He grabs my purse and notebook and helps me into my jacket. We walk quickly to his SUV. Now my head is throbbing.

The drive back to his house is short, but he keeps looking over at me, asking me if I'm alright more than a few times.

"I should be fine. Once it stops bleeding." I give a humorless chuckle. "Ugh. I'm so clumsy sometimes."

We get to his house but instead of pulling into the garage, he stops in front of the door. He turns the engine off and jumps out, making his way to the passenger side. He opens my door.

I take his hand when he offers it to help me out of the vehicle. I can't help thinking about my date with Prescott, when he did the same. Only with him, holding his hand was warm and comfortable. Grabbing Mr. Anderson's hand sends my insides into a frenzy.

He guides me inside and makes me sit on a stool in the kitchen. I wait and watch as he puts some ice into a Ziploc bag, then wraps it in a clean towel. He holds it out to me. "Put this on it."

"I don't want to ruin your towel."

"Forget the towel, Miss Sterling. Put the ice on your head. You've already got a lump." He eyes my head with a frown.

I take the ice and gently hold it to the bump on my head. I close my eyes.

"Shall I make you some soup?"

My eyes open and I look at my employer. "Why, Mr. Anderson," I say, in mock surprise. "Was that a *joke*?"

I swear he nearly smiles.

"Thank you." I refer to the ice.

He nods.

After a moment he says, "You're right, you know."

Chapter 15

I raise an eyebrow.

"You *are* clumsy."

I laugh, then wince because it causes my head to throb again.

"I should get home," I say softly.

"I'm driving you."

"Oh, you don't have to do that." I wave my hand dismissively. "I'll be fine."

"I'm driving you home, Miss Sterling. It wasn't a suggestion."

"Oh. Okay. I appreciate it."

He nods.

As I stand to leave, I watch as once again Mr. Anderson gathers my things for me. Could it be that there is a slight crack in his stony exterior?

I smile to myself as I follow him back out to his SUV. If there's a softer side to Merrick Anderson, I'm definitely ready to discover it.

Chapter 16

When Mr. Anderson pulls up to my apartment, I feel a little self-conscious. My entire apartment could fit in his massive living room. I'm hoping he'll drop me off at the door and leave.

He doesn't.

He parks in the visitor section and gets out. Once again he assists me out of the car, and once again my heart flips when I take his hand.

"Which one is yours?"

"Through here." I point to the door of the building on the right.

He nods and leads me that way. We get to the door and I dig my keys out of my purse. When I look up, Mr. Anderson is staring at my head.

"I'll be fine," I chuckle. "It's already feeling better." I unlock the door to the building and step inside, my boss following me. "It's this one."

He nods, waiting as I open my apartment door. Cinnamon and spice hit our noses as we enter, thanks to the scented oil plug-ins I have in every room. I've also decorated for fall, and while some might call my decorations excessive, I love it.

"Festive," he says.

"Thanks." I take it as a compliment, whether he meant it as one or not.

"You said your dad lives by you?"

I point to my dining room wall. "Right next door."

He nods. "I should tell him what happened."

Chapter 16

"Um, sir? That's not really necessary. You can go if you want. I don't want to take up your whole Saturday."

"You're not," he states. "Besides, I wouldn't mind saying hello to William again. See how he's doing."

I glance at the clock on my microwave. It's just after two. Prescott will be here in less than an hour. I sigh. "Alright. Let's go."

He follows me next door, where I knock softly and call to my dad. "Dad? It's me. Are you decent?" I ask, teasing.

I hear him laugh and tell me to come in, so I open the door.

"You're early," my dad says. Then he spots Mr. Anderson and looks surprised. "Oh! Merrick, hello. I thought you might be Prescott."

"Hello, William. I assure you—I'm not."

Before this gets uncomfortable, I walk over to my dad and kiss his temple. "How are you feeling?"

"It's a good day."

I never get tired of hearing that answer.

"You should be asking Billie how she's feeling, as well."

I look at my boss. I've never heard him call me Billie.

"Billie?" My father looks at me with concern. "What's happened? Are you alright?"

"She has a head injury," my boss answers for me.

I throw my hands up. "Oh, the dramatics," I say, laughing. "It's nothing, Dad, really. I bumped my head at the library."

Mr. Anderson scowls. "You were bleeding."

"Bleeding? Billie!" My dad gets up from the couch.

"I am *fine*!" I motion for my dad to sit back down. "You know how it is when you hit your head. It always looks worse than it is. I'm completely alright. Just a little sore."

"You need to take it easy today," Mr. Anderson orders.

"Thanks, *Dad*." I roll my eyes.

My dad laughs while my boss continues to stare at me, glowering.

"Sit down, both of you," Dad says.

I sit on the couch near my dad's recliner, and Mr. Anderson sits in the other recliner across from my dad.

"Do you want something to drink?" I ask.

"I'd love some water," my boss says.

"Sure." I get up and walk to the kitchen. I grab three bottles of water and return to the living room. "I think I'm going to go next door and make some coffee. Dad doesn't drink it. Would you like a cup?"

Mr. Anderson nods.

"I'll be back," I say.

I walk to my apartment and close the door. I lean against it for a moment and blow out a breath. I can't relax with my boss sitting in my father's living room! I don't even want coffee that badly—I just needed an excuse to get out of there and have a moment to myself.

I get the coffee started, then head to the bathroom. One look in the mirror causes me to gasp. Since my hair is pulled back, I can see the lump on the left side of the top of my head and the dried blood in my hair. I look like a hot mess.

I decide to take a few minutes and wash my hair over the sink. I'm careful not to scrub the bump, but gently wash around it. When I'm done, I blow-dry it quickly. It goes back up in a ponytail and I put on a clean shirt.

When I walk back to the kitchen, I glance at the clock and see I've been gone for fifteen minutes. The coffee is done and thankfully still hot, so I make two cups and head back to my dad's.

As I walk through the doorway, I say, "I'm sorry I took so lo—" but I cut myself off when I see another person has joined my dad and Mr. Anderson.

"Prescott," I say. "You're early." I set the two coffees down on the small table by the door.

"Only ten minutes." He walks up to me and hugs me tightly. I don't know why, but I'm slightly embarrassed at his display of affection. I don't even look in my employer's direction.

"Are you ready to find out what I'm making?" He grins.

I grin back. "Absolutely."

"Cheeseburgers."

I throw my head back and laugh. "One of my favorites."

Chapter 16

"Good." Prescott looks at Mr. Anderson, who is as stone-faced as I've ever seen him. "Merrick, you're welcome to join us for dinner. I've got plenty."

Please say no. Pleeeease say no...

Mr. Anderson nods. "I'll stay."

Great.

"I'd like to keep an eye on Miss Sterling's injury, anyway."

I want to die. Just crawl under the couch and close my eyes forever.

Prescott looks at me, concern covering his face. "What injury?" he demands.

"It's nothing," I say, wishing everyone would forget about the whole thing.

My dad chimes in. "She cracked her head open today."

"Dad! Not the *least* bit true!"

"Mr. Anderson takes his turn. "She's got a nasty bump and I'd like to make sure she doesn't have a concussion."

"*Concussion?*" Prescott grabs my upper arms and looks into my eyes. "Are you alright? Have you seen a doctor?"

I step back, pulling away from him. "Okay, guys, I appreciate the concern, but this is ridiculous. I'm perfectly fine. Yes, I hit my head. Yes, there was a *little* blood. But I. Am. *Fine*."

I walk into my dad's kitchen and turn to Prescott. "What do you need for dinner?"

All three men are looking at me.

"Okay, look. I'm not lying when I say I feel fine. If I get dizzy, or nauseous, or... *whatever*, I promise I will say something. But please, just believe me when I say that I'm alright!"

"Sorry, Pumpkin."

Prescott smiles. "Yeah. Sorry, Pumpkin."

Mr. Anderson says nothing.

"Ugh!" I spin around and grab a frying pan from the cupboard and set it on the stove. "Here—if you need anything else, my dad can tell you where it is." I walk over and grab my coffee cup and sit on the couch near my dad.

This evening is going to be *so* fun.

***

"Answer… come on, Anne, answer."

I stare at my phone until I see my cousin's face appear on the screen. "Oh, thank God," I say. "Are you busy?"

She flashes a perfect white smile and her little dimple appears in the corner of her mouth. "Not too busy for you. What's up?"

I flop back on my bed, my hair splaying around my head. "Men." I roll my eyes. "I just had the most bizarre evening."

I see the excitement on Anne's face as she gets close to the screen. "Do tell."

I laugh. Then I tell her about the first part of my day, including my injury. "How romantic!" she squeals.

"Romantic? What in the world is romantic about all of this? It was humiliating!"

"You were injured and two handsome men were fighting over who was going to take care of you," she breathes, dreamily.

"Anne. Having to run back to my apartment to wash the sticky blood out of my hair was in no way, shape, or form romantic. And I'm pretty sure the only reason Mr. Anderson cared at all was because I got injured while working with him. He probably doesn't want to get sued."

Anne continues to giddily look at me, and I swear I see tiny hearts in her eyes. I know that every word I'm saying is going in one ear and right out the other.

I continue on anyway. "And *then*, Prescott invited Mr. Anderson to stay for dinner and he accepted! Talk about awkward. And Prescott made some pretty great burgers, but Mr. Anderson ate them with a look on his face that said he'd rather be eating anything else. I really don't know why he stayed." I roll my eyes again. "The only person that acted remotely sane tonight was my father."

Anne laughs. "Your social life is so much better than mine right now."

"Be serious!" I say, laughing. "I don't know what to make of all this." I shake my head. "I have an attractive, genuinely nice guy who's interested in

Chapter 16

me, but I just can't seem to think of him romantically." I pause. "Then I have an attractive boss who is about as easy to figure out as the Great Pyramid and I'm trying to *stop* myself from thinking about him romantically."

"I knew it!" Anne yells into the phone. "I knew you liked your boss!"

I'm surprised it doesn't hurt her to grin that hard.

"I don't know, Anne. It's not like I think he's even interested in me, but… well, it's hard for me to even let my thoughts go in that direction, because he seems to be bitter at God for some reason. And that bothers me. You know how important my faith is to me."

"Yeah, I know. Have you tried talking to him about it?"

"No. He avoids the subject at all costs."

"Hmm."

"What are you thinking, Anne?" I ask suspiciously.

"Nothing…" she says, but I don't believe her for a second.

I sigh and tell her I'd better hang up. We both have to be up early for church.

After we say good night, I lie on the bed staring at the ceiling.

Lord, this is getting super complicated. I don't want to find myself having feelings for someone who may never reciprocate them. I also don't want to begin a relationship with someone who doesn't want a relationship with You. Lead my heart in this.

As I let my eyes close, I think about the day and how it ended. Prescott wants to go out again. I really need to let him know that I just want to be friends, but I know it won't be the easiest thing to do. I truly don't want to lose his friendship… and I don't want to risk hurting him.

Even though these are my thoughts as I lie here, a certain dark-haired, brown-eyed boss is on my mind when sleep comes to claim me.

Chapter 17

It's been a week since I hit my head. Thankfully, my boss didn't make a big deal out of it and only asked once that following Monday if I was alright. I gave him an angry glare and he didn't ask again.

This last week flew by. Mr. Anderson and I have been so busy with this ball that there hasn't been much time for me to sit and think about these new feelings. But that didn't stop my heart from racing every time Mr. Anderson leaned over my desk to show me something on the laptop or ask me for information. I don't think I'll ever smell pumpkin spice again and not think of him.

I have, however, managed to avoid Prescott. He's called me several times and I've let it go to voicemail. I've just texted him back saying that I'm super busy and I'll call him when I can.

Now it's Saturday afternoon, and my phone is ringing. I need to answer and get this over with.

"Hey, Prescott."

"Billie!" I can hear the relief in his voice because I've finally answered. "How are you?"

"I'm good. Just been busy."

"I figured."

"What about you?" I ask.

"Same, although maybe not as busy as you." He laughs.

Chapter 17

"It's just this ball. We have a little over a month and still so much to take care of. We still haven't heard back from the boys' choir. I'm getting a little nervous and thinking I need a back-up plan."

"Merrick is lucky to have you."

"Thanks."

There's silence for a moment, then finally Prescott says, "I don't want to be in the way, Billie."

"What?"

He sighs. "I don't know if I'm just imagining things, but it seems to me there may be something between you two."

I get flustered. "There's... nothing, I mean... there's nothing going on. He's my boss."

Prescott laughs. "Billie, anyone that's in the room more than two minutes with the both of you can see that there's a mutual attraction there. I don't want to get in the way of that."

I'm quiet for a moment. Boy, I got thrown into *this* conversation sooner than I was ready.

Finally, I say, "I'm not going to lie to you, Prescott. I'm not exactly sure what I feel yet, but there is definitely *something*. I do want to say, though, that I've loved getting to know you and spending time with you. I truly enjoy your company."

"Just not romantically."

"Not romantically," I say softly.

He's quiet now, and I can't help feeling a little awkward.

"I've enjoyed getting to know you, too, Billie. I'd love it if we stayed friends."

I laugh in relief. "I'm so glad to hear you say that."

"Well in that case, as a *friend*, would you accompany me to a costume party tomorrow night?"

"A costume party?" I laugh.

"Yeah. It's kind of a big deal."

"Oh?"

"Yeah. My niece is turning sixteen, and since her birthday is so close to Halloween, she wants a huge costume party complete with prizes for the best costume. My sister asked me to be a chaperone of sorts. Keep an eye on all those sixteen-year-old boys who think they're God's personal gift to all the young ladies."

I laugh loudly. "And you need an extra set of eyes?"

"Are you game?"

"Definitely. It actually sounds like fun."

"Great. How about I pick you up around six? It starts at seven, but they live about forty-five minutes away."

"Sounds good. Wait! What do I wear? I don't just have costumes lying around."

"No pressure," he says. "You can just make something you have work."

"What are you dressing up as?"

"Jack Sparrow."

I laugh again. "I love those movies."

"Me too."

"I'll figure something out."

Once we hang up, I give a quick prayer of thanks. *Lord, that was easier than I thought. Thank You for guiding me through that smoothly.* I'm thankful it didn't get awkward.

Well, not *too* awkward. There was still the part where Prescott pointed out my attraction to Mr. Anderson. Oh, Lord. Is *everyone* noticing?

* * *

"Dad, can I borrow your brown long-sleeved shirt?"

"Sure. Can I ask why?"

"I need it for a costume I'm making. I'm going with Prescott to his niece's birthday party."

"Ah. Still seeing Prescott?"

"Yeah. As friends."

"I see."

"Dad."

"Hmm?"

Chapter 17

"Don't read too much into anything."

He smiles. "Of course not, Pumpkin."

I shake my head. "So, Anne's coming by tomorrow evening to hang out with you, huh?"

"Yep. She and your aunt Rosie are going to make me dinner."

"Nice." I'm glad someone will be here with him.

He hasn't gotten any worse these past few weeks, but with the treatment no longer working, I know it's only a matter of time before he starts to go downhill. I'm dreading that day. But in the meantime, he wants me to keep living my life. It kills him to think I'll cancel plans or put them on hold for him. I'm thankful for family and friends who step up and help me keep him occupied. If he didn't have them, I *would* be putting my life on pause.

I'm headed to his room to grab the shirt when I see mail on the counter. I can't help but see it's a medical bill. One for over three thousand dollars. I thank God once again for this job. With the money I'm making now, I can finally start to pay some of these down.

I keep walking and don't let my dad know I've seen the bill. He feels bad as it is, having to rely on my income for the both of us. I don't mind. Taking care of my dad isn't a burden to me, but I know at times he feels like it is.

I grab the brown shirt from my dad's drawer and head back to the living room.

My dad is staring at his phone, frowning.

"Dad? What's wrong?"

"It's nothing."

I walk to his side and glance over his shoulder.

I see a picture of Mr. Anderson and a tag that reads, *The temperature isn't the only thing getting colder...* The person goes on to rip Mr. Anderson apart for refusing to plan an event having to do with a group of social elitists who are known to exclude anyone from their affairs who makes less than half a million a year. But of course they spin it to paint him in the worst light they can—even accusing him of being jealous of their social standing.

"What a load of garbage," I say angrily. "They're so unfair to him. I've worked with him nearly a month now and I've learned some things about him that would put these people to shame. He's one of the most charitable…"

I trail off and my dad stares up at me, eyebrows raised. "A little defensive of your boss, aren't you?" I can tell he's trying not to laugh.

I playfully swat his shoulder. "I just think he's being misjudged, that's all. And I don't understand why he doesn't defend himself to these… these *people*."

"Maybe it's not worth it to him. People are going to think what they think, regardless of what proof they may have otherwise."

"True. I just wish I knew what happened to make everyone hate him."

"Why don't you google it?"

I laugh. "*I'm* supposed to remind *you* to use technology, not the other way around. I can't believe I didn't think of it." I pause. "But… is that invasive, do you think?"

"Nah," my dad says. "It's obviously public knowledge. *We* just don't know the details."

"You're right," I say. But I can't help feeling like digging into my employer's past *is* a bit intrusive. But would he answer my questions if I asked him about it? I doubt it.

But still… before the night is over, my curiosity may just get the best of me.

* * *

I decide against coffee tonight and heat some water for tea. I settle on the couch with my cup and my laptop.

I'm a little nervous at the thought of what I might find. The truth is, I really am starting to like Mr. Anderson and I'm not sure if the negative things I might read will change my opinion of him. I know that seems unfair—no one wants to be judged by their past. But I'm a little afraid I might read something that *will* cause me to look at him in a different way.

I blow on my tea and take a small sip. Then I set it on the coffee table and get online.

I type "Merrick Anderson" in the search and hit *enter*.

Chapter 17

There are several articles about his business and the charities he's helped. But they're not what stands out. There's a headline that catches my attention and I click on it.

I see a picture of Mr. Anderson next to a beautiful dark-haired woman. She's got deep brown skin and perfect cheekbones. She's tall and has a flawless figure. And Mr. Anderson has his arm around her.

I feel a tiny twinge of jealousy at the intimate pose. Okay, more than a tiny twinge. A humongous twinge. I wonder who she is.

Read the article, Billie.

Oh. Duh.

I learn that the woman's name is Sophia Denmark. She was Mr. Anderson's partner—and girlfriend, apparently. *Key word here is WAS, Billie,* I tell myself.

The article goes on to say that Mr. Anderson cheated Miss Denmark out of her half of the business. That he used "unethical tactics" to misguide her and "pull the wool over her eyes."

I frown. Mr. Anderson may be cold and rude, but he doesn't strike me as devious or unethical. The rest of the things written about him are so nasty I don't even finish the article. I hit the "x" in the corner and close out of the browser. I shut my laptop and set it aside. That's enough research for tonight.

Help me understand this, Lord, I pray. *Help me find the truth here and not jump to conclusions. And if there are deep hurts on Mr. Anderson's part, please heal them and bring him back to you.*

I've found myself praying for my boss a lot lately. I know there is something there that I just haven't figured out—haven't been able to piece together. But I'm also beginning to see that God definitely has me there for a reason and I need to let Him work through me.

Then I think that with a boss like mine, it may not be the easiest thing to do.

Chapter 18

When Prescott shows up at almost exactly six o'clock, I'm ready. I open the door and can't help the grin that spreads across my face when I see his detailed Jack Sparrow costume. "You look awesome," I say. "Very piratey."

"Thanks," he laughs. "Okay, so, you're... a monkey?"

I'm wearing brown from head to toe, my hair is slicked back into a tight bun at the nape of my neck, and I followed a makeup tutorial on how to paint your face like a monkey. I even attached a tail to my pants.

"I'm little Jack," I say. "The undead monkey."

Prescott throws his head back and laughs. "This is *great*. You look awesome."

"Thanks." I know this is going to be a fun night.

The ride to his sister's is a pleasant one. Prescott makes great conversation, and it's nice to feel so comfortable with him, knowing that there are no expectations other than friendship.

We make good time, arriving at 6:40. Prescott takes me into the backyard where it's set up exactly how you would imagine a teenager's Halloween costume party. There are lighted lanterns and bowls of candy. There are fall-colored streamers everywhere. In the corner of the yard is a "photo booth" made of bales of hay and pumpkins. Music is blasting from a wireless speaker.

Chapter 18

I meet Prescott's sister, Penny, and her husband Will. They're dressed as Fred and Wilma Flintstone. Penny is greeting the teens coming into the backyard, pointing out a huge punch bowl filled with a grayish liquid and telling them to help themselves.

"Where is your niece?" I whisper to Prescott.

"Penny, where's Nicole?" he asks.

"Just finishing her makeup—she should be down soon. Wait until you see her." Penny grins.

"I can imagine," he laughs.

We don't have to wait long. Nicole walks out of the sliding glass door a moment later. She is absolutely the most beautiful teen version of Strawberry Shortcake I've ever seen. Her hair is long and hot pink. She's got on white and green striped leggings and red high heels. She's wearing a little cupcake as a hat. And her makeup is stunning. She looks like a glamorous doll. Good looks certainly run in Prescott's family.

"Oh my gosh, your niece is adorable," I say.

He grins. "I know. Now to keep all these hormonal young men at a reasonable distance," he jokes.

At least I *think* he's joking.

The party turns out great. There are about thirty sixteen-year-olds all dressed up, trying to impress the guest of honor. She ends up picking her three favorite costumes: a boy dressed up as the guy from the game Operation, a girl dressed as Frodo Baggins, and a really creepy kid that looks frighteningly like a ventriloquist dummy. She gives them all gift cards to the local mall.

Prescott and I stand off to the side, eating Halloween-themed finger foods and watching all the teens trying to impress the opposite sex. Prescott makes a comment about us never being that bad when we were their age, but I assure him we were.

Then we watch Nicole open her gifts. She gets a variety of things, ranging from a Bluetooth speaker pillow to a set of car seat covers that look like unicorns. Prescott informs me that she received a car from her parents yesterday.

"Ah," I say. "Nice."

I give her a warm smile as she thanks me for the bath set. I had a difficult time deciding what to get a young girl I'd never met, but I didn't want to come empty-handed. She seems to genuinely like it, so I'm happy.

By about 9:30 we're ready to go. We say goodbye to Penny and Will, and they thank me for coming. Then we say goodbye to Nicole and she hugs me.

"It was sooo nice of you to come, Billie. I hope Uncle P brings you around more often." She grins at Prescott.

"We'll see, Nikki." He hugs her.

When we climb into Prescott's truck, I turn to him and smile.

"That was actually *really* fun," I say. "Thanks for bringing me along. Your niece is a riot."

"Yeah, she is. My whole family is pretty great."

"*You're* pretty great, Prescott," I say. "And I know God has someone for you who will suit you perfectly."

He smiles. "Thanks, Billie. I believe that."

I start laughing.

"What?" he says.

"It's just that I'm thinking about the woman who could love you dressed as Jack Sparrow."

"Hey!" he laughs. "Maybe I'll wear this to church next Sunday to impress the ladies."

"And I'll wear *this* to work tomorrow and watch Mr. Anderson faint dead away."

Prescott smiles but doesn't laugh.

"I'm sorry. Does it make you uncomfortable when I talk about my boss?"

"No. I'm just hoping he comes to his senses soon, in more ways than one."

"Oh?" I say softly.

"I've been praying for him lately, Billie. And I have a feeling you have, too."

"Yeah," I agree.

"I just hope he mends his relationship with God before he tries to start one with you." He glances at me. "You deserve the best version of Merrick, Billie. And what you see right now is not it."

Chapter 18

I turn to look out the window as he drives, and I think about what he said all the way home.

* * *

I'm already in a great mood when I walk into the office the next morning, but what I smell when I stand by my desk delights me. Apple cinnamon. I twist around to look at the outlet on the wall beside my desk and I see it. A scented oil plug-in.

"Sir…" I start, slowly turning and grinning. "Was this you?"

Mr. Anderson never looks up from his laptop but says, "Yes."

"Thank you. I love it."

"Don't thank me; thank Margaret," he says. "She brought over a bunch of those things and they're overwhelming my home."

I walk to his desk and lean on it with my hand. "And was it Mrs. Joy that happened to remember that I *love* scented oils, especially cinnamon spice?" I give him a look that says I'm on to him.

Never moving his head, his eyes lift to meet mine. "I was assaulted by spices the moment I walked into your apartment, Miss Sterling. How could I forget?"

"Now you can be assaulted by cinnamon every time you walk over to my desk." I grin.

"I'm not paying you to stand here and chit-chat, Miss Sterling. I need you to call those numbers I left on your desk. I noted each one."

I stand straight and salute him. "On it, sir!" I turn and walk to my desk.

When I get there, I glance at my boss. Not even a hint of a smile. Obviously, I've forgotten about his no-sense-of-humor policy. I roll my eyes and make the first call.

* * *

I'm finally done with my sticky note phone calls. I gather them and hold them up. "Do you want me to keep these?"

No," my boss says. "I have the numbers saved."

I shrug and toss them in the garbage.

"So, any plans for Halloween, sir?"

"No."

"You mean you don't hand out candy to all the cute little bumblebees and fairies?"

"No."

"Ugh. I wish I could hand out candy, but we're not allowed in our complex. You've got this great house in a busy neighborhood. What a waste." I shake my head. "I miss seeing all the cutie-pies dressed up."

"Be my guest, Miss Sterling."

"Huh?"

"You're welcome to stand at my door and give away candy," he says, never looking up from his screen.

"Really?" I say, delighted. "You wouldn't care?"

"Not at all. Just don't count me in."

"I wouldn't dream of it," I say. "It's probably for the best, anyway. Even without a costume, you'd scare the children with your scowl."

He looks up and glares at me.

I laugh. "Do you mind if I bring my dad along? I try to get him out of the house whenever I can. This will be perfect—he can sit in a chair and still get to see all the kids."

"Of course," he says.

"And what will you be doing while we're passing out candy?"

"Working."

"Why did I even ask," I mumble, turning back to my desk.

"Miss Sterling, do you remember calling a Jerome Whitaker?"

"Um, yes, I think so. From the printing company?"

"Yes. Please give him a call back and let him know we'll be going with his company for the cutouts."

"Sure thing," I say. "Best prices, huh?"

"That, and I found out he's a huge supporter of our area's Special Olympics. Therefore, I'd like to support him."

Chapter 18

I smile. There it is. Another glimpse inside the real Merrick Anderson. I want so badly to ask him about the article I read, but I'm not sure of the response I'll get and I don't want the rest of the day to be awkward. Besides, I'm not sure I'm in the mood to hear about *Sophia Denmark*. I roll my eyes.

"Something wrong, Miss Sterling?"

Great. He barely looks in my direction ninety-nine percent of the time, and he happens to look over at this moment.

"No, sir," I say. "Just thinking about something I read yesterday."

He looks at me for a few seconds, but as usual, I can't tell what in the world he's thinking. He finally turns back to his computer.

I make the phone call to Mr. Whitaker. We work out all the details and he lets me know how happy he is to have our business. When we end the call, I realize it's lunchtime.

"I'm taking my lunch," I say. "Would you like me to bring anything back for you?"

He thinks for a moment and then finally says, "I'll just go with you."

Um.

"Oh. Alright," I say, trying not to show my surprise.

But boy, am I surprised. Mr. Anderson never leaves for lunch unless it's work related. Then I think that perhaps he wants to talk about the ball or something. I sigh. I *really* just wanted to enjoy my lunch today.

I grab my jacket, purse and keys. "I'll drive?" I offer.

He nods.

I grin.

He's just going to love the harvest spice air freshener I just got for my car. It's new... and still nice and strong.

I lead the way and he follows me outside.

Chapter 19

Mr. Anderson says nothing as he climbs into the passenger seat of my Fiesta, but I know he notices the scent. However, I quickly forget about that as I see him squeezed into my little car. His head nearly touches the ceiling.

I try not to laugh as I start the car. And I don't suggest that we take one of his vehicles, because I'm enjoying the prospect of driving *him* around for once.

"Where do you want to go?" I ask.

"Clark's?"

"Perfect. I love their burgers."

We drive for a moment in silence, then I finally say, "So, you want to discuss the ball?"

"Why do you say that?"

I shrug. "I just figured if you're coming to lunch with me, you want to discuss work."

"You'll never stop assuming, Miss Sterling, will you?"

"I have to assume with you, sir. You never tell me what you're thinking."

He looks out his window and mumbles, "You should thank me for that."

I roll my eyes. "You're not the villain everyone says you are. And you don't have to pretend to be, either. At least not with me," I add quietly.

"Do you always listen to what everyone says about me, Miss Sterling?"

Chapter 19

"No," I say truthfully. "I'd rather hear your version."

"My version of what, exactly?" His voice is icy.

Oh, shoot.

"I've just… seen some articles," I say.

"I see."

"But I know the media isn't fair to you."

"Don't pity me, Miss Sterling. I'm not the least bit affected by what the media says about me. Or anyone else, for that matter."

"Well, there are some people that actually care about the truth," I say softly. "I'm one of them."

Mr. Anderson says nothing.

We pull into Clark's and get out of the car. I see my boss stretch and I grin.

It's self-seating here, so I choose a booth in the corner. We settle in and look at the menus they keep at each table.

A super bubbly, cute blond waitress comes over to take our order and she gives Mr. Anderson a huge smile. "Hope you folks are doing well today. What can I get for you and your lady?"

"Um, I'm not his lady," I say quickly, my face flaming.

Her grin widens. "Oh. Do you want separate bills?"

Before I can respond, Mr. Anderson says, "No. One is fine."

"Oh," Miss Bubbly says again. "Well, who wants to start?"

My boss gestures for me to go first, and I order a burger with mushrooms and an order of fries.

"To drink?" she asks.

I'm tempted to order a coffee but decide against it. "I'll just have water, thanks."

"Got it." She turns to Mr. Anderson and the grin is back. "And for you, honey?"

His stone face doesn't flinch as he orders a double bacon burger and onion rings. Miss Bubbly says that it'll be right up. Then she *winks* at him.

Eye roll.

It's funny how the man sitting across from me can look as if he's ready to rip someone's head off, yet the women that cross his path still swoon and giggle, trying their best to capture his attention. I notice he doesn't even glance in her direction as she walks away.

"So. Tell me about this article."

"Um… article?" I ask.

"You're too smart to play dumb, Miss Sterling."

I sigh. "It was this article online about you and some woman." I shrug as if it doesn't matter.

"Some woman?" He quirks an eyebrow. "Are you referring to Miss Denmark?"

"I guess that was her name." I wave my hand dismissively.

And what did the article say?"

"Something about your business and your breakup."

"Oh?"

"Yeah."

Silence.

"I was seeing Miss Denmark for a while," he says after a moment.

"I figured."

"I broke it off when I saw a side of her I didn't like."

"Oh."

Our waitress sets our waters down and tells us our food should be ready any minute. I take a sip of my water and look up at Mr. Anderson.

"The article said she was your partner."

He frowns. "Partner is a generous word. She did nothing for my company except what benefited her." He picks up his own water and takes a huge drink.

"It also said that you cheated her out of her half of the company," I say quietly.

He stares at me. "And do you believe them, Miss Sterling?"

Miss Bubbly breaks into our awkward conversation by bringing our food to the table.

When she walks away, Mr. Anderson surprises me by telling me to pray over our meal. I do. And I'm much more comfortable praying in front of him this time than the last.

Chapter 19

When we begin to eat I simply say, "No. I didn't believe them."

Mr. Anderson nods.

We eat for a few moments in silence before I ask, "Did you ever try defending yourself?"

He stays silent, chewing his food.

"I mean," I continue, "I don't know everything that happened, but if their version is wrong, why didn't you put out a statement or do an interview or *something*?"

"You're right, Miss Sterling. You don't know what happened." He takes another bite.

"So tell me."

"How is everything tasting?" our waitress asks. I didn't even realize she'd walked up to our table.

"Fine," my boss answers, without looking at her.

She seems a little disappointed that her flirting hasn't worked on him yet. "Well," she says with a forced smile, "is there anything else I can get for you?"

"No, thank you," I say, and my smile is genuine. I swear it has nothing to do with the fact that she's gorgeous and my boss is ignoring her.

She nods and walks away.

"So?" I ask.

He continues eating, and I wonder if he's deciding if he wants to tell me the whole story. I don't want to pressure him into sharing or make him feel uncomfortable. I'm just about to change the subject when he speaks.

"Four years ago, we were hired to plan a benefit for Down syndrome awareness. It was a statewide event, so they needed help planning for such a large number of people."

"I remember hearing about that event," I say. "In Lansing, right?"

He nods. "Sophia's little brother Shane has Down syndrome, so this was an event particularly important to us."

"Oh," I say quietly.

He takes a deep breath and continues. "There are two sides to Sophia—the side that adores Shane and would do anything for him…" He pauses.

"And?"

"And the extremely selfish side that would go to any length to make herself look good." He scoffs. "The two sides seemed to be warring constantly."

"So, what happened?"

"We were working together to make this the biggest and most successful benefit we'd ever done, and it looked like it would be. Then she went behind my back and started working for a man who promised her that she and Shane would be the new faces of a campaign for Down syndrome."

"Oh no…" I say softly.

"She was way too tempted by the thought of getting famous through this campaign, and without consulting me, handed over nearly our entire budget to this man who promised to 'get them started.'"

I raise my hand to my mouth and close my eyes.

"Obviously, I learned very quickly what she had done, and instead of trying to make it right, she made excuses for herself and hung on to the prospect of becoming some kind of spokesperson for this campaign. I suddenly became the bad guy for trying to hold her back. She accused me of being selfish and cheap."

"Oh my gosh," I say, shaking my head.

"When the committee for the benefit found out our budget was gone, they dismissed us. Fired us, I guess you could say. Sophia never once told the truth about what happened, and since I had founded the company, she let me take the fall for everything."

"Why didn't you say something?" I ask. "Tell your side?"

I see something in Mr. Anderson's eyes that I've never seen. *Hurt.* "I loved Shane," he says sadly. "I didn't want to destroy him by exposing his sister. He was such a happy guy and Sophia genuinely cared about him. I didn't want her or Shane dragged through the mud over her stupid choice. I don't care what people think about me, but I wanted to protect Shane."

My heart nearly bursts. *He's a good man.*

"So," I ask, cautiously, "What became of you and Sophia?"

He scowls, and I wonder if I should've left it alone.

"I broke everything off with her—our relationship, the business… church."

"Church?" I ask, surprised.

Chapter 19

He looks at me and his brown eyes are as cold as ever.

"Sophia was my pastor's daughter."

Oh. So much makes sense now.

"They took her side?" I ask.

He shakes his head. "No, actually. I did get to explain to her parents what had happened. They were pretty ashamed and upset." He shrugs. "I guess that was another reason I didn't go to the press with my side. They would've ripped Pastor Denmark and his wife to shreds. I didn't want that."

I can feel a tear in my eye and I quickly blink it away. "I'm so sorry you went through all of that," I say sincerely.

"It's not your fault, Miss Sterling." He begins eating again.

I take a bite of my own burger and chew slowly, thinking. Finally, I ask, "So you never found another church to attend?"

He looks up at me, his face hardened. "Let's just say I needed a break from *church people.*"

"And you thought you'd take a break from God, as well?"

"I believe that's none of your business."

I hold my hands up defensively. "Sorry."

We continue our meal in icy silence until I say, "I'm glad you told me."

He just looks at me, chewing.

"Really," I say. "I know that can't be easy for you to talk about. But I'm glad you did. I told you that I didn't believe you were the villain the press makes you out to be."

"I expect you to keep what I've shared to yourself, Miss Sterling."

"Oh, trust me. I wouldn't *dream* of letting on that you're anything but a sticky-note-obsessed workaholic who is allergic to smiling." I grin at him and shove a few fries in my mouth.

Then I nearly choke as I see the corner of his mouth tip up slightly.

Chapter 20

It's Thursday afternoon. The morning was busy and I'm thankful things have calmed down since before lunch. I've been wanting to tackle Mr. Anderson's desk again. That man doesn't need a whole lot of time to mess up his space. It looks like I'll have to clean it at least once a month to keep it from driving me absolutely crazy.

My boss isn't back from lunch yet, which is unusual. Normally, he's back at his desk before I am—that is, if he actually eats his lunch somewhere other than his desk. Oh, well. I decide to get a head start on cleaning.

I make my way to his desk and start organizing. I gather some papers that I know need to be kept together. I reach for a paper clip, but the container is empty. Sighing, I head to the storage closet.

I reach for the knob and twist it, pushing the door open. There stands my boss, looking intently through a stack of papers.

"Mr. Anderson! I didn't know you were here."

He looks up at me, then back at his papers.

"Looking for something?" I ask.

"Yes."

"Can I help?"

"I doubt it."

"Okay, then."

I quickly find the extra office supplies and grab a handful of paperclips.

Chapter 20

I leave the storage room and place them in the empty container on Mr. Anderson's desk.

I'm clipping the stack of papers together when I hear the door open and my boss's voice say, "Miss Sterling."

I turn, and he motions for me to come back to the storage room. I follow him back to the stack of papers he's looking through and he holds his hand out toward it.

"Maybe a fresh set of eyes *will* help."

"Sure," I say. "What are we looking for?"

He holds up a sheet of paper that looks like an invoice. "There's another one of these and I need them both."

I take the paper and study it for a few seconds so I know what I'm looking for. Then I grab a small stack of papers and begin sorting through it.

For a few moments, the only sound in the quiet room is the shuffling of paper. Then suddenly my boss asks, "Are you ready for tomorrow?"

"Tomorrow?" I ask. *Uh-oh. What am I forgetting?*

"The candy," he says.

"Oh, right." Tomorrow is Halloween. "Yeah. I actually have a ton of candy. I might be here all night passing it out," I jokingly threaten.

"It's fine," he says, never looking up from his papers.

Oh. My heart skips at the possibility of him *wanting* me to be at his home.

We're both quiet again. I'm through with my stack of papers and reach for another.

"How are things going with Prescott?"

His question shocks me. I mean, *really* shocks me. Of all the things to ask me, that was the last question I'd expect.

"He's becoming a great friend," I say.

For a brief moment he stops shuffling through his papers and looks at me. But he quickly gets back to it and says casually, "Friends? It seemed like you were both quite interested in each other."

I feel my face burn. "We really hit it off," I admit. "We have a lot in common. We just…" I let my voice trail off.

Mr. Anderson turns to me, a slightly amused look on his face. "You just *what*, Miss Sterling?"

He's enjoying making me uncomfortable!

We stand there in the storage room staring at each other. He's waiting for an answer; I'm wishing he'd drop it.

Finally, I say, "I just don't feel… *that way*… about him."

He puts his paper down and steps closer to me.

"*What* way?" he asks, his voice low.

I swallow. *He's so doing this on purpose!*

"You know!" I say, flustered.

He stares at me for a moment, and I would give just about anything to know what he's thinking. "I think I *do* know… Miss Sterling."

I stand there holding my stack of papers, looking at him. Really looking at him. It's so quiet I can hear my own pulse and I can't look away from my boss. For the first time, I see something in his eyes that isn't ice. It's more like… *fire*.

I quickly look away and I can feel my face flaming. I start shuffling through the papers once again, not really remembering what it is I'm looking for. Mr. Anderson calmly goes back to his search as well.

About thirty seconds go by when I come across a paper and something clicks. It looks just like the one he showed me.

"Ah! Here you go," I say, and my voice sounds awkward in my own ears. It's a hundred degrees in here and I just want to get out and go back to cleaning the desk. I hold the paper out to him.

He takes it and nods.

I turn and leave. I don't even chance a look behind me because I can feel him watch me as I go.

* * *

I load the candy into my car and turn back to the apartment building just as my dad is walking out.

"Dad!" I say, laughing loudly. He's dressed like the painter, Bob Ross. And he looks *fantastic*. "You look amazing!"

Chapter 20

He grins and does a little painter's pose, putting his fist to his chin like he's trying to decide what to do next.

"Get in the car," I say, still laughing.

We both climb in and are buckling our seatbelts when he says, "You look pretty great yourself, Pumpkin."

"You think so?" I smile. I'm dressed as a cute scarecrow. I have on dark jeans and brown fuzzy fall boots. My red, brown, and dark orange flannel shirt has tiny bits of straw sticking out from the sleeves, neck, and buttons. On my head is a feminine floppy straw hat, and I've painted my face in the most adorable fashion.

"It's been a while since we've gotten to do this, huh?"

"It sure has," my dad answers.

As we pull out of the complex, I say, "Dad, can I ask you something?"

"Always."

"Do you think someone who's been hurt in church—or by church people—can get over it and eventually come back?"

"Whoa. That's a meaty question."

I laugh a little. "It's just that I found out that Mr. Anderson used to be involved in a great church with what seems like a great pastor, but he was hurt deeply by someone in the church he was close to. He hasn't gone back since and it doesn't seem like he cares to, even now."

"Ah. I knew there was something," he says. "And are you worried about falling for someone who doesn't share and practice your faith?"

I shrug. "I can't lie to you, Dad. My feelings for him are definitely… changing."

"I see. And you've been guarding your heart because of this whole thing."

"Yeah," I say softly. "I don't want to be in a relationship where faith is only important to one of us. I've seen it tear couples apart." I pause. "I want a relationship where God is the center."

"And you should," my dad says, putting his hand on my arm. "Put it in God's hands, Pumpkin. Trust Him."

"I'm trying," I say truthfully.

"As for your question—absolutely. I believe anyone can make their way back. Keep praying for him, and I will too."

"Thanks, Dad." I smile at him. "That means a lot."

We drive in comfortable silence until we pull up to my boss's. I park in my usual spot in the front and grab the candy bags from the back seat. My dad takes one from me and we walk to the front door. The sun is setting, but I don't see kids out in the neighborhood yet.

"We made it in time." I knock on the door.

Mr. Anderson opens it a moment later and steps back so we can come inside. Gone are the starchy work clothes I see him in every day. He's wearing dark gray sweats and a light blue t-shirt. His hair is slightly messy from changing clothes and he looks *adorable*.

"Um, hi again," I say, awkwardly. "Uh, do you have a big bowl?"

"I should," he says, turning to walk to the kitchen.

"I'll be right back," I tell my dad. "You can sit down if you want." I point to a small bench by the door.

My dad sits; I take his bag of candy and follow Mr. Anderson into the kitchen.

When I get there, he's already rummaging through the cupboards. I set the bags of candy on the counter and begin opening them. I have a great variety and want to mix them all in one bowl for the kids to grab.

"Ah," my boss says. "Here we go." He pulls out the biggest Tupperware bowl I've ever seen and brings it to me.

I laugh at the huge white bowl. "Why do you even have this?"

"My mother used to sell Tupperware."

"That explains it."

"And there's a lot more where that came from," he says dryly.

"A mother's son can never have too much Tupperware," I say in mock seriousness.

He's staring at me now and it just dawns on me that I'm dressed up as a scarecrow. Since he's made no room in his life for fun, he must think I look ridiculous. I blush.

"Uh, let me get this candy out there before the kids start coming." I begin pouring the bags into the bowl. "Oh, and could you make sure your porch

Chapter 20

light is on, please?"

He nods and walks toward the front door.

I take a moment and mix the candy around in the bowl so the kids can see every kind. Then I head to the front porch to sit with my dad.

When I step outside again, I see that Mr. Anderson has set chairs out for us. *Three* chairs. And he's sitting in one of them.

"You're not working tonight, sir?"

"I may put in an hour or two later," he says. "But right now, I want to see you two in action."

"Oh. Okay." *This won't be weird at all.*

I can see a few families down the street headed our way. I sit in the chair and wait.

A mom with a little red-haired girl that looks to be about two years old approaches the porch. She's dressed as The Little Mermaid, which is perfect because she doesn't even need a wig.

"Go ahead," the mom coaxes her.

The little Ariel walks shyly up to me and says, "Ticker-tee."

"Ooohhh, you are adorable!" I hold the bowl of candy down where she can reach it. "You take a nice big handful," I say, smiling.

Grinning, she digs her tiny little hand into the bowl but can only grasp three pieces. I wink at her and grab a handful and drop it into her seashell bucket.

"There you go," I say. "Have fun!" I wave as she runs back to her mom.

"Thank you," the mom says to me, and they head to the next house.

I sit back. "Oh, I've missed this."

A few other kids dressed like superheroes come up and get their candy.

After a little while, a girl about four years old steps up onto the porch, her eyes fixed on Mr. Anderson. She's dressed as Tiana from The Princess and the Frog, and she looks remarkably like her. She's even got a little stuffed frog attached to her shoulder. I hold out the bowl of candy, but she walks right past me and stands directly in front of my boss.

Mr. Anderson leans forward with his arms resting on his knees and says, "Hello."

"Hi," the little girl says.

I'm assuming that the older girl that steps forward is her sister. "Jordan, don't bother the man."

"It's alright," my boss says.

Jordan reaches up and places both little hands on the sides of Mr. Anderson's face. "Where's your costume?"

"I don't have one."

"Why?"

"I just don't."

"Because you're handsome enough?"

Mr. Anderson does something I've never heard him do. He laughs.

I look over at him and he's actually *smiling*.

And he's gorgeous.

Chapter 21

"You should do that more often," I say to Mr. Anderson after the little girl and her sister leave for the next house.

"Do what?"

"Smile. Laugh." I shrug. "It looks good on you."

"Oh?"

My dad stands and asks where the restroom is. Mr. Anderson tells him and Dad slips inside, leaving me and my boss alone.

A few more kids make their way up to the porch for candy and then it's quiet for a few moments.

"I was serious," I say quietly. "Smiling has never hurt anyone."

Mr. Anderson just sits there, looking at me intently.

My dad comes back out at that moment and asks if he can see me inside. I step inside and he closes the door.

"I'm sorry Pumpkin, I know we just started handing out candy, but I'm not feeling well."

I notice his face is pale and I start to panic. "Oh, gosh, Dad! What's wrong?"

"No, no, don't worry. I just need to get home and rest."

"I'll take you right now."

I open the door and Mr. Anderson is filling the candy bags of two little twin boys, both dressed as Spiderman. "Sir, I'm sorry, but I've got to take my dad home. He's not feeling up to staying all night."

When the boys walk away, he stands. "I know how much you were looking forward to tonight, Miss Sterling. I could take your father home if you'd like."

I glance at my dad, unsure. "I don't know…" I say. "Do you need me?"

Dad shakes his head. "No. No, you stay, Pumpkin. You love this."

"Okay," I say. I look at my boss. "Thank you."

He nods.

Dad, if you need me for *anything*, call. I'll come immediately."

"I know you will." He kisses my cheek. "Have fun."

"I will." I watch them leave.

I'm sitting alone for a few minutes when three kids with homemade costumes approach the porch. The oldest looks about ten or eleven, and he's wearing a robot costume made of boxes and dryer hoses. The next is a girl about nine and she's a scarecrow like me. The youngest looks around five and he's dressed like a classic hobo from the old movies, complete with smudges of "dirt" across his face.

The girl speaks first. "Hi! Wow, this house *never* passes out candy."

Her older brother nudges her. "Shhh!"

I laugh. "It's alright," I say. "It *has* been a while."

"It's just that we're surprised to see someone here handing out candy," the older boy says. "This house is usually dark and quiet on Halloween."

"Well," I say with a grin, "this is my boss's house. I'm here because I can't pass out candy where I live."

The little hobo's eyes get wide. "No candy?"

"Not a piece," I say. "So, Mr. Anderson—he lives here—gave me permission to hand out my candy from his porch. Wasn't that nice of him?"

"Yeah!" the kids say in unison.

I smile and hold out the bowl. "Help yourselves."

The kids politely take one piece each.

"Aw, you guys can do better than that," I laugh. "Grab a handful."

The siblings all look at each other for approval, then grin as they dig their hands in.

"That's more like it!" I say.

Chapter 21

"Thank you, miss!" the girl says.

"You're very welcome. Have fun!" I wave as they head back down the sidewalk.

* * *

After about a half hour of handing out candy, I see my boss pull into the garage and I stand as he gets out of his car and comes to the porch.

"How did he seem?" I ask a bit anxiously.

"I think he's more tired than anything," he says. "It doesn't seem like anything serious."

I sit. "Okay," I say, relieved. "I just get so worried lately. Any day now, everything could change."

Mr. Anderson sits too and continues to look at me. "He's worried about you."

"Me?" I'm surprised. "Why? I'm perfectly fine. He's the one dealing with all this. I'm afraid that he's often in pain more than he lets on." I shake my head. "Why would he worry about *me*?"

"He's worried about how you'll be when he's no longer here."

Wow. Blunt, much?

I swallow, blinking back tears. It's dark and I'm thankful he can't see them. "I'll be fine. It's his life being cut short. I'm not selfish enough to think about how *I'll* be when he's..." I can't say it.

"Miss Sterling," he says, "you're the least selfish person I know. It's *okay* to think about yourself sometimes."

His words surprise me. I just look at him, not knowing what to say.

Finally, desperate to change the subject, I ask, "What about your parents?"

"*My* parents?"

We're interrupted when a mom, dad, and young girl walk up the sidewalk. The foot traffic more than slowed down. And it's a good thing, because I'm finally running out of candy. A quick peek down both directions of the street tells me that this may be the last trick-or-treater. I dump the remaining ten or so pieces of candy into her pillow case and smile.

"That's it," I say. The girl thanks me and waves bye.

"Well," I say to my boss, holding up the huge bowl, "let me get this inside and wash it. You never know when you'll need to make pasta salad for thirty people."

He nods, and without laughing at my joke begins to gather and fold up the chairs. He follows me inside and I flip off the porch light. I make my way to the kitchen while he takes the chairs to the garage.

In no time, I've got the bowl washed and I'm putting it back in the cupboard I remember Mr. Anderson pulling it from. I turn around and he's standing in the doorway, watching me.

The evening is over, and suddenly feeling a little self-conscious, I pull my floppy straw hat off my head. I know I've still got the black triangle on my nose and the rest of the makeup that makes me a scarecrow. I can't imagine what he thinks.

I start pulling the straw out of my sleeves and neck and toss it in the garbage. "So, you got out of *that* question pretty easy," I say.

"What question, Miss Sterling?"

"When I asked about your parents." I sit on one of the stools at the island counter.

He walks to me and sits on the stool next to mine and faces me. "My parents," he says, "live in Pennsylvania. They run an antique shop and they're very good at what they do. They can spot an authentic antique in a junkyard from half a mile away."

"Nice," I say. "Do you see them often?"

"No."

I wait for more. He says nothing.

"No? As in, it's difficult?"

"No, as in, I don't really make the effort." His frown deepens. "And neither do they."

"Oh," I say sadly. "That's too bad." I swallow hard to keep my emotions in check. "I can't imagine what it would be like to have both of my parents alive and healthy, and *not* want to see them as often as I could."

Mr. Anderson is quiet, but he continues looking at me. I still can't guess

Chapter 21

what he's thinking and I still wish I could.

After a moment, he says, "Maybe you're right."

I gape at him. "I am?"

"I probably should make more of an effort to see my folks."

"You... you should," I agree. *Did Mr. Anderson really just admit that I'm right? I should log this and timestamp it.*

My phone buzzes in my pocket and I pull it out. "It's my dad," I say. "Give me a second."

I answer. Dad doesn't sound good.

"Are you coming home soon, Pumpkin?"

"I'm leaving right now," I say, standing and reaching for my keys. "What's wrong?"

"I'm not sure."

"I'll be right there." I hang up and shove the phone back in my pocket. "I have to go. Something's wrong."

Mr. Anderson stands as well. "Is there anything I can do? Do you want me to drive you?"

I lay a hand on his arm and look up at him. "Thank you, but no. I'll be okay. I promise, if I need something, I'll call."

He nods and I'm out the door.

* * *

I'm trying to watch my speed. I'm trying not to panic. I'm trying to pray.

The fifteen-minute drive home is seeming like fifteen hours. Every moment that goes by is a new opportunity for a thought to bombard my mind—for me to worry.

I pull in, park in my spot, and make my way to the building door. I fumble with my keys and drop them. While I bend to pick them up I feel the tears coming. I open the door and walk to my dad's apartment. It's unlocked.

"Dad?" I call.

"In here."

I walk down the hall to the bathroom. He's sitting on a fold up chair next to the toilet. "Dad! What's going on?" I can't hide the panic in my voice.

"I've been throwing up blood," he says, and winces. He holds his stomach. I can tell he's in pain.

"I'm taking you to the hospital. Right now."

He doesn't argue. And that scares me.

I tell him to wait on the couch and I go pack a small bag for him. Pajamas, toothbrush—the essentials. Then I head to the living room and tell him I'll be right back.

"I'm going next door to pack my own bag," I tell him. "I'm staying with you."

"Pumpkin, you don't have to—"

"Don't argue. I'm staying. I'll be right back."

I leave and quickly let myself into my own apartment. I grab some essentials for myself and a book and shove them in a bag. I take twenty seconds in the bathroom and wash the scarecrow makeup off my face. I'm back in my father's apartment in less than three minutes.

"Let's go," I say. "Where's your jacket?"

He points to the front closet and I grab it for him. He's already got his shoes on so I pick up his bag and walk out. I lock the door behind us.

We get to the car and I make sure he's situated before I walk to my side and get in.

"Okay," I say. "Let's go find out what's going on in that stomach of yours."

"I'm pretty sure it's cancer." My dad's attempt at a joke.

"Dad," I say quietly. "Please don't."

"What?" he asks, and out of the corner of my eye I see him looking at me. "Don't talk about reality?"

I stare ahead at the road. "You're going to be okay," I whisper.

"Pumpkin," he says softly.

I don't want to talk about this anymore, so I tell him I need to call my boss. I pull my phone out and ask him to pull up the number, since I'm driving. He does.

It rings only twice and Mr. Anderson answers. "Miss Sterling." His voice is laced with concern.

Chapter 21

"Hi," I say. "I just wanted to give you a heads up. I won't be in tomorrow. We're on our way to St. Mary's."

"Oh no," he says.

"Yeah," I agree.

"Take all the time you need."

"Thank you. I appreciate it."

"Of course." There's a pause and then, "Tell your father I'm pulling for him."

"Sure."

We end the call and I burst into tears.

Chapter 22

My dad sleeps as I read my book in the uncomfortable chair they graciously set out for friends and family. It's 2:00 am but I couldn't sleep if I tried.

This is the turning point. My dad is not going to get better. He is going to die.

I have no tears left to cry. I'm dried up. The doctor was as gentle and caring as he could be, but the words he spoke couldn't be sweetened with any amount of sugar. *It's time to make him as comfortable as we can.*

Dad told me that we'd have Christmas together. I guess I got used to the idea that he'd still be around for a while. I'm just not ready. I'll never be ready.

* * *

I wake up with a terrible pain in my neck. I fell asleep in a weird position and must've slept that way for hours. The last time I remember looking at my phone was about 4:35. It's now 7:50. A nurse is taking my dad's blood pressure.

"Good morning, Sleeping Beauty."

I grin at my dad. "Morning." I yawn. "I need coffee."

The young nurse smiles. "If you go down right now to the cafeteria,

Chapter 22

everyone is getting their morning coffee. That's a good thing because they're making it fresh every few minutes."

"Gotcha," I say. "Thanks."

I walk to my dad and kiss his temple. "Do you want anything?"

"No, thank you."

"Alright. I'll be back." I grab my purse and phone and head down to the cafeteria.

The nurse was right. It's pretty busy, but the staff is doing a great job keeping the lines moving.

Once I get my coffee and add my cream, I find an empty table by the window and sit for a few moments. I pull out my phone and check my notifications. There's a text from Anne.

OMG keep me posted. PRAYING

I had texted her last night to let her know what was going on, but she must've been sleeping because she didn't answer until early this morning. I decide to wait to text her back until I've talked to the doctor about our plan from here on out.

I check a few emails for no other reason than to get my mind off of things for a few minutes. But nothing seems important at the moment and I just skim over them, not really paying close attention.

I put my phone away and stare out the window. *Lord,* I pray silently, *I can't do this without You. I need you right now. Help me deal with whatever comes. And help me trust You.*

I drain my cup, throw it in the trash and head back up to my dad's room.

The doctor is here. He wants to explain to me what's going on, and what to expect from now on.

I'm not ready.

But I swallow hard and nod to him.

My dad needs an at-home nurse. I have the option to find someone on my own or they can help recommend someone.

The doctor goes on to explain the details of what to expect in these last four weeks. *Four weeks. That's all I have with my father.*

The doctor continues speaking—I can tell this because his lips are moving.

I hear nothing else but the roar of the ocean, like someone has held up huge seashells to my ears. My pulse is thumping and skipping and I start to feel funny.

I begin to struggle to draw in a breath. *Oh, God, help me. I can't breathe.*

I'm shaking and sweating, and I hear the doctor shout for someone. The young nurse is at my side in a moment, helping me to sit. She's saying something.

"...panic attack, Billie."

"What?" I look up at her and blink. My chest hurts and I place both hands to it. "What?" I ask again.

"I said, I think you may be experiencing a panic attack. It's okay. We're going to calm down."

Calm down? I want to push her away from me. My father is slowly being ripped away from me and I'm supposed to *calm down?*

"Deep breaths, Billie."

I realize now that I'm sucking in quick breaths like someone is snatching the oxygen from me and I'm trying to get in all I can before it's permanently taken from me. I close my eyes.

"That's it... slow, deep breaths."

I feel a paper towel on my forehead and notice the nurse is mopping the sweat from my face.

"I can't do this," I whisper, shaking.

"Billie, come with me." The nurse stands and holds out her hand.

I take it and follow her out of the room. She leads me into a family lounge area, and thankfully it's empty, giving us some privacy. She sits me in one of the chairs and tells me she'll be right back.

She reappears a moment later with a styrofoam cup of ice water and hands it to me. I suddenly realize how thirsty I am and take it gratefully.

She sits next to me and places a hand gently on my arm. "Billie, you are going to be alright," she says.

I look at her, my eyes flooding with tears. "I don't see how," I croak out.

She takes my hand and looks me right in my watery eyes. "I've had a few great conversations with William," she says. "And I found out that we share

Chapter 22

something very special and important."

My brows rise in question.

"Our faith."

I attempt a smile.

"Billie," she continues, "none of this has caught God by surprise. He hasn't left you yet and He won't leave you now."

The reality of her words hits me hard and the tears spill. "Thank you," I say, and I reach over and hug her fiercely.

"I want you to sit here for a few moments," she says. "Try to calm down. Keep breathing slowly and deeply. Drink your water. And remember who's in control." She squeezes me and then lets go.

I nod to her. "Tell my dad I'll be back in a few."

She smiles. "I will." Then she walks out of the lounge.

I take advantage of having the room to myself and spend some time in prayer. I *have* to trust my Heavenly Father. I know it's the only way I'll make it through this.

I'm about to head back to my dad's room when a thought hits me. I need to talk to someone. I wonder if Anne is busy. I pull my phone from my pocket and scroll through the numbers.

But it isn't Anne's number I find.

I hit send and wait. After a few rings I hear the voice that is oddly comforting.

"Miss Sterling."

"Hi," I say to my boss. "I hope I'm not bothering you." My voice sounds off, even to my own ears.

"Not at all. How's William?"

I break. I tearfully tell him everything. I don't know why I chose to call him over my cousin and best friend. I just did. And now I'm unloading everything that's piled up on my shoulders.

He listens. When I'm through, he says, "I'm coming up there."

I feel a bit guilty and say, "Oh, you don't have to do that. I just needed to… vent, and well, I guess you were the one I chose to unload on." I give a humorless chuckle. "Sorry."

"Don't apologize. I'll see you soon."

He ends the call.

What did I just do?

* * *

A little less than an hour later, my boss walks into my dad's room. And he's got Mrs. Joy with him.

I get up from my chair and make my way to them, and Mrs. Joy pulls me into a hug. "Honey," she whispers in my ear.

I feel her tenderness toward me and blink the tears away. I can't answer her just now for fear I'll start sobbing.

Mr. Anderson walks to the side of my dad's bed.

"Well, William, can't seem to stop causing trouble now, can you?"

My dad laughs and that lightens my mood a bit.

"Merrick. Thanks for coming by, but it wasn't necessary. You're a busy man."

"I have nothing to do that can't wait," Mr. Anderson says. "Besides, I have a bit of business here."

"Oh?" My dad raises an eyebrow.

"William, I'd like you to meet Margaret Joy. She's worked for me for years and there's something you need to know about her."

Now *I'm* curious.

Mrs. Joy steps forward and smiles at my dad. "It's nice to meet you, William. And what Merrick was trying to say is that I am a retired nurse."

"I hear you're going to need someone to stay with you—Margaret is perfect."

I stare at my boss, gaping.

"What in the world?" I say.

Mrs. Joy turns to me and smiles. "Surely I've mentioned this to you?"

"Um, no," I say.

"Oh, sorry, dear." She waves her hand dismissively. "When Merrick told me what was going on, I couldn't stand by and let a stranger move into your

Chapter 22

father's home. Not when I'm capable of helping out."

I try to say something, but my voice sticks in my throat.

Mr. Anderson speaks instead. "William, Margaret is a widow whose children are married with families of their own. She works for me to have something to keep her busy."

"May I ask why you retired in the first place, then?" my dad says.

"Of course. About seven years ago, my daughter was in a bad car accident and sustained quite a few serious injuries. She had a baby and a toddler at home. I retired early and took care of them for the better part of a year. When she no longer needed me, I decided to find work that was slightly less stressful than that of a busy hospital." She sighs. "Now, don't get me wrong—I love nursing. I just decided that this young man—" she pats Mr. Anderson's shoulder, "needed a little help, and it might be a nice change of pace for me." She shrugs. "So, here I am."

"But I have decided that I can spare her for a time," my boss says in a tone that dares to be argued with. "So, if you agree, William, we can see about getting her started in your home. She'll be a live-in nurse as long as you need her."

I can't stop the tears. This is just too much. It's happening so quickly and I need some time to process it all. Mrs. Joy, my father's *nurse*? I excuse myself and leave the room.

I head down the hall, back to the family lounge, praying that I can be alone. I step inside and see that God has answered my prayer. I walk over and stare out the window, reminding myself to breathe. Slow, even breaths. I don't want to have another panic attack. Not now.

I'm looking out the window and counting my breaths when I sense someone else enter the lounge. I don't want to turn around and see who's here. I just want to be alone.

But then I can feel that the person is close to me and I turn to see my boss standing right behind me. I open my mouth to speak, but I'm cut off when he reaches for me and crushes me to his chest.

Chapter 23

By the time I pull away from his embrace, I've soaked Mr. Anderson's starchy white shirt.

I brush at it with my fingers. "Sorry," I say sheepishly.

He gently cups my chin and tips my face to look up at him. "Don't apologize."

"You—" I hiccup. "You didn't have to do that, you know."

"I'm aware of that. And for the record," he says, "I'm not in the habit of doing things I don't want to do. No one *makes* me do anything."

I nod, hiccupping again.

"Listen," he begins, guiding me to a chair. He sits next to me. "I know you'll want to spend as much time as you can with your father. But I also know that you can't take care of him yourself. Margaret will take a huge load off your shoulders. You can enjoy your time with him rather than stress over the small things. She's a great caretaker."

I nod again. "I can't thank you enough," I say. "I'd like nothing better to do than to stay home with my dad every minute until…" I stop myself from saying it. "Anyway, I just don't think it will be good for either of us. I'll need some time for myself and I know he will." I look at my feet.

"I don't expect you in the office any time soon, Miss Sterling."

I look up at him. "I can't afford to miss that much work," I say softly.

He nods. "Understandable."

Chapter 23

"I'll spend as much time with my dad as I can in the evenings and weekends."

He nods again.

I take a deep breath. "Thanks again… I don't know how I can ever repay you."

Mr. Anderson looks at me intently and opens his mouth to say something when two older women enter the lounge and sit near us. Mr. Anderson closes his mouth.

"Were you going to say something, sir?" I ask quietly.

He stares at me for a few seconds then shakes his head. "It can wait."

We stand, and my boss follows me back into my dad's room. He and Mrs. Joy are chatting away, both of them smiling.

Mr. Anderson leans close to me. "Looks like they're hitting it off pretty well."

"Yeah," I say, smiling. "Thank God." I would never want my dad to be uncomfortable with his caregiver.

They notice us standing by the door and Mrs. Joy laughs. "Billie, you didn't tell me your dad was such a charmer."

I roll my eyes and laugh. "He tries to be," I say.

My dad waves Mr. Anderson over. My boss stands next to the bed and Dad holds his hand out.

"Thank you," he says, shaking Mr. Anderson's hand. "You're a good man."

Mr. Anderson nods his head but says nothing.

"Well," Mrs. Joy says, standing to her feet. "Let's get these details worked out."

* * *

It's Sunday evening, and my dad is resting comfortably at home. His living room looks like a hospital room. It makes me a bit sad, but I know he's a lot more comfortable sitting here than in an actual hospital.

Mrs. Joy has been fantastic. Once a nurse, always a nurse, I guess. She's jumped right back in there like she never retired. She's the perfect person to take care of my dad. She's stern when she needs to be, but she's compassionate.

I'm folding a load of laundry when I feel her hand on my shoulder. I turn to her.

"Billie, you haven't been home yet. You need to take a little time for yourself. I can get William settled." She takes the shirt from my hands. "Besides, what will I have to keep me occupied if you do all the housework?"

I smile. "Thank you, Mrs. Joy. I think I *will* go home. I need a shower and my own laundry needs to be caught up."

I give her a quick hug and grab my things. "Dad, I'll be back in a little while."

"Get some rest, Pumpkin," Dad says. "You didn't take more than a cat nap at the hospital. We'll be fine." He winks at Mrs. Joy. "I won't give Margaret too much trouble."

"I guess I could use a little nap," I say.

My dad wags his finger and tries to look stern. "I don't want you taking *just* a nap. In fact, I don't want to see you until tomorrow."

"Dad," I begin.

"No," he says, holding his hand up to stop me. "I mean it. In fact, you go to work tomorrow, and I'll see you in the evening." He grins. "You can cook me dinner."

Mrs. Joy squeezes my shoulder. "We'll be fine, honey," she says, and I can tell she means it.

"Okay, okay. You guys win," I say. "I'm going sleep the night away and then work all day and not even *think* about you," I tease.

"Attagirl," my dad says. It's good to see him in a lighthearted mood.

I enter my apartment and throw my purse over my recliner. I go to the stove to heat up some water for tea, then I collapse on the couch. I'm mentally and physically exhausted.

I pull my phone out of my pocket and see I've got a text from Prescott.

Hey, you. Thinking about you and your dad. Hope things are getting better. Still praying.

I smile. I'm thankful for his friendship. I send a text back thanking him and giving him a quick update, then I set my phone aside and get up to make

Chapter 23

my tea.

I leave my tea on the counter to steep and take a quick shower. Just being clean feels wonderfully relaxing. I take comfort in knowing my dad is on the other side of the wall, and if there is an emergency I can be with him in seconds.

After throwing a load of laundry in, I settle back on the couch with my tea and a blanket. This is the first time I've been alone with my thoughts in days.

I begin to pray. I don't know how long I sit there, pouring my heart out to my Father and crying, but it's a while. When my tears dry, I grab my Bible off the coffee table and open it.

I turn to one of my favorite comforting passages, Psalm 27. *"The Lord is my light and my salvation—whom shall I fear? The Lord is the stronghold of my life—of whom shall I be afraid?"*

I inhale a deep breath through my nose and slowly and gently blow it out. "I won't be afraid…" I whisper. "I won't be afraid."

* * *

I sleep the entire night without waking once. When I look in the bathroom mirror, my eyes are puffy.

Great.

I wash my face with cool water and tie my hair back in a ponytail.

I look at the clock. 6:27. I decide I can't wait until I'm at the office to have my coffee today, so I make a small pot. I sit at my little dinette and try to decide whether to stop by my dad's before I leave. I decide not to. I don't want to start my day as an emotional wreck, and that's what I'm afraid will happen if I go next door.

I take my time getting ready, choosing a casual dress outfit and flats, because I just want to be comfortable today. I look in the mirror, and even though I've looked better, I'm satisfied that I won't be going to the office resembling a troll. I grab my coat and purse.

I arrive at work before eight o'clock. I walk in the front door and smell coffee. Mr. Anderson probably assumes I'm not coming in today. Smiling, I head up the stairs and open the office door.

"Good morning, sir," I say.

"Miss Sterling," he says, looking up from his desk.

"I needed to come in today." I make my way to my desk and put my purse in the bottom drawer.

"I understand."

I hang my coat on the rack by the door—the rack I picked up a few weeks ago. "Did you have your coffee yet?"

"No."

I nod. "I'll be right back."

I walk down to the kitchen and can't help but notice how quiet things seem without Mrs. Joy here. I wonder how she and my dad are doing this morning and decide that I'll shoot my dad a text a little later to ask.

I pour two mugs of coffee and add cream to mine, and cream and sugar to Mr. Anderson's. I head back upstairs and set his on his desk. I turn to walk back to my own desk when my boss stops me.

"Miss Sterling."

I turn. "Yeah?" I take a sip of my coffee.

He looks up at me and after a moment asks, "How are you doing?"

I lean on his desk with my hand and sigh. "I'm alright," I say. "Just trusting God to get me and my dad through this."

"Trusting God," he says, flatly.

"Yeah," I say. "Trusting God."

He stares at me for another moment and I have no clue what he's thinking. Then he says, "To each their own, I guess."

I set my cup down on his desk and cross my arms, but it has nothing to do with the ever-present chill in the office. I'm aggravated.

"Sir," I say, "I don't know why you're so bitter at God. I know what you went through was hard, but this blaming God thing is childish and silly. Or maybe your faith was weak in the first place, that it could be so easily shaken."

I don't know why I said it. It just kind of came out.

In a second, Mr. Anderson is on his feet, looming over me, causing me to

Chapter 23

have to tip my head back to look at him. The desk is behind me and I have nowhere to move, so I just stare up at him.

"You have no idea what you're talking about. You don't know *anything* about the condition of my faith or anything else."

"It... it just kills me to see you so angry at God," I whisper.

He's even closer now, and when he speaks, his own voice is quiet.

"Is that why you were so eager to get to know Prescott? Because he's got strong *faith*?"

This catches me off guard. "I—I..." I don't know how to answer.

"Don't go with him."

"What?"

"Don't go to the ball with him, Billie." He whispers. "Go with me."

Um.

I slip myself out from between him and his desk and hurry over to my own. I sit in my seat, my heart pounding. Then I glance over and realize I've left my coffee.

Mr. Anderson sees it too and picks it up. He walks over to me, his eyes never leaving mine, and sets it down in front of me.

"Thank you," I manage to squeak out.

Expecting a nod, I'm surprised when he says, "You're welcome."

We're just looking at each other, and even though I'm a bit uncomfortable, I can't look away.

"I was serious, Miss Sterling. I'd like you to go with me."

I don't know why I say it, but it just comes out. "Okay."

He nods, a satisfied look on his face.

I swallow hard and watch him walk back to his desk.

I grab my laptop and turn it on.

What in the world just happened?

Chapter 24

What have I done?

What am I going to tell Prescott?

I can't believe I agreed to attend the ball with my boss. It's like when he asked me, all rational thinking went out the window. I just said "okay" like I had no other plans in the world.

I pull up to my complex and into my space. I turn off the engine and just sit there, thinking. I don't know if I've made a mess of things, made things complicated, or just made a bad decision. *Did* I make a bad decision? I shake my head. I need to talk to my dad.

Gathering my things, I step out of the car and close the door. I hit the lock button on my key fob and head inside. Stopping first in my own apartment to change, I put on blue exercise pants and an oversized Mackinac Island t-shirt. After checking a few emails and answering two texts, I head next door.

My dad is sitting on the couch with his ugly afghan and Mrs. Joy is lounging in the recliner next to him. They're watching one of my favorite Jimmy Stewart movies, *The Shop Around the Corner*.

"I love this one," I say, smiling.

"Hey, Pumpkin," Dad says. "Come join us."

This seems like the perfect thing to get my mind off of the day, so I plop down next to Dad on the couch. "What, no popcorn?"

Chapter 24

My dad rubs his stomach and shakes his head, making a sour face. I forget that he's not eating much lately.

I shrug. "Oh, well. I remember where your candy stash is," I say.

"Wait, there's a candy stash and I haven't found it yet?" Mrs. Joy says, feigning anger.

I laugh. "In the cupboard above the stove there's a canister marked 'receipts.'" I scrunch my nose and shake my head. "There are no receipts in there."

"Hey!" my dad protests. "Now you're giving away all my secrets."

I stand and kiss the top of his head. "I'm sure Mrs. Joy will keep your candy secret." I head into the kitchen, laughing.

After the movie is over, Mrs. Joy goes to the kitchen to pull a roast out of the oven. It smells wonderful. I meet her in the kitchen and speak low, so my dad can't hear.

"Has he been eating?"

She shakes her head. "Not much," she whispers, concern filling her face.

"The doctor says that's normal," I say, a grim look on my face. "But I'd still make him a plate, just in case he takes a bite or two."

She nods and makes him a small plate.

We gather back in the living room. He doesn't even have a table anymore—it's been moved for a bed. He's now sleeping in the dining room, and Mrs. Joy is staying in his room.

We pray and begin eating—well, Mrs. Joy and I eat—and I work up enough courage to talk to my dad about what's going on.

"So," I say between bites. "I, uh, decided that I'm attending the military ball with Mr. Anderson."

Mrs. Joy is about to put a forkful of food in her mouth, but stops, lowering her fork to her plate. "Oh?" she asks, quietly.

"You look about as surprised as I did when I told him yes," I say, laughing nervously.

My dad is just listening.

"He, um, told me not to go with Prescott, and asked me to go with him, instead."

Mrs. Joy smiles as she takes a bite. Dad smiles, too.

"Oh, I see you both are happy about this."

They look at each other and their smiles get bigger.

"Wait, wait, *wait*," I say. "What's going on here?"

"Nothing," my dad says innocently, shrugging.

"No," I say, "that look wasn't *nothing*. Spill, both of you."

Mrs. Joy sighs, but she's the one to offer an explanation. "We just think you and Merrick would get along just fine."

"Get along just fine? What is this, 1950?"

Both Mrs. Joy and my dad laugh.

I cross my arms, waiting for an explanation.

Mrs. Joy suddenly turns serious. "For the last four years, I've watched Merrick withdraw from the world and sink lower into his cold life of isolation. He doesn't even see his family anymore." She shakes her head. "I don't know what it was, but since that first day you came knocking on his door, I've watched the iceberg that is Merrick Anderson slowly begin to melt."

My jaw drops slightly as I listen to her. It's hard to picture my boss warming to anything, let alone that thing being me.

"I've seen the way he watches his clock in the mornings, and I'm fairly certain he's counting the minutes until you arrive." She smiles at me. "I do believe, Billie Sterling, that you've had quite the impact on our boss."

"I knew from the moment I met him, he was completely taken with you," my dad says.

"Oh geez, guys," I say, shaking my head. I have no idea how to answer that.

"Does Prescott know you have feelings for Merrick?" Mrs. Joy asks me, like it's the most natural thing in the world.

"Um, yeah…" My face is red, I can feel it. I hate that my feelings are exposed like a billboard on the freeway.

I decide to be honest. I feel like they can both see through me if I'm not, anyway. "I really don't know what's happening here. I *do* have feelings for Mr. Anderson. But I don't want a relationship with someone who doesn't share my faith."

Chapter 24

Mrs. Joy comes and sits next to me, putting her arm around my shoulder. "He *does* share your faith, Billie."

I turn to look at her. "He does? But he... I mean, I—"

She smiles and pats my hand. "He's just lost his way. Perhaps you're the one who can help him find it again."

* * *

Mrs. Joy's words are still echoing in my head when I get to work the next day.

I've just settled in at my desk after giving Mr. Anderson his coffee. When the phone rings, I answer.

"M.A. Planning, how can I help you?"

"Hello," says a woman's voice. "This is the office of Merrick Anderson, correct?"

"Yes, it is. Can I help you?"

"Maybe. Is he in? I'd like to speak to him, if possible."

I glance at his desk to make sure that he's not on another call. "Of course," I say. "May I tell him who's calling?"

There's a pause, and then a soft "Sophia Denmark."

I freeze, and for a split second I can't think of what to say. Then I manage to get out, "One moment," before hitting the *hold* button.

I stand and walk to my boss's desk. "Excuse me, sir?"

He looks up at me.

"Sophia Denmark, on hold," I say.

He looks at me for a moment with no expression, then he nods. He waits until I'm back at my desk to pick up.

He answers in a low voice, and I do my best to not eavesdrop. Afraid I won't be able to ignore the conversation, I take this moment to make a quick trip to the restroom, where I spend a few moments checking my hair. It's first thing in the morning, and I'm still nearly perfectly put together, but it gives me something to do that doesn't involve wringing my hands at my desk until Mr. Anderson ends the call.

When I get back to my desk, he's already hung up the phone and he's typing. After a moment, I hear the printer, so I go gather the papers for him and set them on his desk. He mentions nothing about the phone call.

Not that I expect him to. It's not as if he's going to say, *"That was my ex, Billie, but don't worry. There's absolutely nothing between us now, and I told her never to call me again."*

I roll my eyes at my own ridiculous thoughts.

Once again, I find myself wishing Mr. Anderson weren't so hard to read. I also wish he weren't so confusing. Yesterday, he's leaning over me, talking me into attending the ball with him instead of with the charming, well-mannered gentleman I'd already agreed to go with. I say yes, and this morning he's as distant as ever.

And men say women are hard to understand. I shake my head and get back to my work.

* * *

It's lunchtime, and I'm sitting in my car. I've still got ten or so minutes before I have to be back, so I pull out my phone.

Mrs. Joy answers right away.

"Billie. I'm glad you called."

Uh-oh.

"You are?" I ask nervously. At this point, she could have anything to tell me.

"Yes. Now, I don't want to alarm you, but I can't get your dad to eat a thing. I've gotten him to sip some nutrition shakes, but that's it."

I know this is not good news. "Do you remember the last time he ate?"

"Sometime yesterday morning," she says, "and it wasn't much."

I sigh. "Thanks for letting me know. How's he doing other than that?"

"He's sleeping now. He tried to watch a movie but barely lasted ten minutes."

"Alright. I'll be there after work. Is there anything I can bring home?"

"He's been wanting juice."

Chapter 24

"I'll pick some up."

"Okay, thanks, Billie."

"Of course."

We end the call and I slowly exhale. This is it. These are the changes the doctor told me about. But I don't understand why it's happening so quickly. I assumed we wouldn't see these signs for weeks.

Feeling a bit overwhelmed, I step out of my car and head upstairs. I want nothing more than to head home and snuggle up with my dad and a cheesy Don Knotts movie. I want to make popcorn and hear him complain about how it's not salty enough. I want to laugh with him and forget that we ever heard those awful words… *it's cancer.*

Oh God, I pray. *I need You today, I need You now. Give me the strength to make it to 5:00.*

I push open the door and head back to my desk, dreading the next four hours.

Chapter 25

The next week is an emotional roller coaster. For every good moment, my dad has two awful ones. He's thrown up blood at least once a day, and he'll only drink liquids. Mrs. Joy is doing a great job keeping his cup full of crushed ice. He's on a lot of pain meds, and I pray that he's comfortable.

It's Friday evening, and I've only been to work three days this week. I can't think about the money now. Spending time with my dad takes priority.

However, when I log into my banking app that evening, I see that a full week's pay has been direct deposited. I sigh. I've got to fix this before I forget. I pick up the phone and pull up Mr. Anderson's number.

He answers like he always does. "Miss Sterling."

"Hi," I say. "I just wanted to let you know that there's been a mistake on my paycheck this week. I only worked—"

"It wasn't a mistake," he says, cutting me off.

I'm confused. "But I didn't—"

"It *wasn't* a mistake, Miss Sterling. I paid you for the whole week."

"Oh," I say quietly. "Why?"

He's silent for a moment, then says, "Sick days."

"Sick days," I repeat.

"Yes. Sick days."

"But I wasn't sick," I say, and I know he can hear the smile in my voice.

Chapter 25

"Your dad was."

"You'd better be careful, sir," I tease, "or some people may just start to think you're a sweetheart."

"What about you?" His voice is low and quiet. "Do *you* think I am?"

Um.

"I think it was very sweet of you to give me sick days on my father's behalf," I say. "It's much appreciated."

He's quiet and I picture him nodding. It almost makes me giggle.

"How is he?" my boss asks.

I sigh. "It's what you'd expect at this stage. We're just trying to make the most of his time left, and make sure his pain never gets worse than uncomfortable." I swallow. "It's hard."

"I can imagine."

"Sir, I want to thank you for being patient with me having to miss so much work."

"It's not a problem," he says.

We're both silent for a moment, and I tell him I'd better go.

"Have a good weekend, Miss Sterling."

"You too, sir," I say.

When we end the call, I'm smiling.

* * *

It's Saturday evening and I'm staying with my dad overnight. Mrs. Joy is home, taking care of some personal things. I'm kind of glad for the time alone with Dad, but I've gotten used to seeing Mrs. Joy every day and I do miss her being here with us.

I pull two grape popsicles from the freezer and sit down on the couch. I hand Dad one and open the other. He's been on a popsicle kick lately, but I don't mind, because at least he's getting fluids.

"So," I begin, "How are things going with Mrs. Joy?"

My dad smiles. "She's great. I couldn't have asked for a better nurse. And she's good company, too."

"I'm so glad," I say. "I still can't believe it was Mr. Anderson's idea."

"He's a good man, Billie."

"I know."

"No, I don't think you do."

I look at him, confused at his remark. "What do you mean?"

"Billie, did you know that he's still paying Margaret as if she's still working for him?"

My hand covers my mouth. "No," I whisper.

"I knew he most likely didn't tell you, but I think you should know."

"Why would he do that?"

Dad shrugs. "Margaret told me that the day you called him and told him what was going on, he came right to her and proposed the idea of working here instead of there. She said that he told her that since she'd be staying here, he'd double her salary."

"Oh my gosh." I shake my head in disbelief. "I don't understand why…" I let my voice trail off.

"Because he cares, Pumpkin." He places his hand on mine and squeezes. "Margaret was right, you know."

"About?"

"I believe God is using you to bring that young man home." He smiles, but it's weak. "Don't give up on him."

"I won't," I say softly.

My dad gives my hand another squeeze. "How about a movie?"

I agree. It's about all my dad has the energy for, and I know that he most likely won't be able to stay awake for the whole thing. But I choose one anyway, and we settle in for the evening.

* * *

An hour and forty-five minutes later, the movie's over and my dad wakes up.

"Did I miss it?" he asks groggily.

"Oh yeah," I say. "You were out before Dorothy saw the yellow brick road."

He attempts to laugh, but it's more of a silent shake of his shoulders. His

Chapter 25

energy is gone. He asks for a cup of water, and when I get back with it, he takes the tiniest sip, then sets it down and turns to me.

"Pumpkin, I don't want you to worry about anything."

I feel a weird sensation in the pit of my stomach. It's dread. I don't want to have this conversation.

He goes on anyway. "Chuck's been over here a few times to help with arrangements, and so has your aunt Rosie. I don't want everything dumped on your shoulders. I've tried to make things as easy as possible for you."

"Dad," I begin. "I don't want you worrying about all this, I—"

He holds up his hand. "Stop. It will give me peace just knowing that things are taken care of. It's going to be hard enough on you."

"Daddy," I whisper, scooting over next to him and laying my head on his shoulder. He feels so thin. "What am I going to do without you?"

He smooths his hand over my hair and I can feel it tremble slightly. "You're the best thing that ever happened to me, Pumpkin. I'm so thankful God gave me all these years with you."

I can't stop the tears as I sit on the couch with my dad, trying desperately to hold on to the moments we have left.

We cry and talk, laugh and pray. It's a precious night, one that I'll remember forever.

Two days later, my dad slips away peacefully in his sleep.

* * *

There is a huge difference between living with a piece of your heart missing and having a piece of your heart ripped out.

Growing up, I never had a mother. I always felt like I was missing out on something that all the other kids had.

But having something precious for so long and having it taken from you is a whole different kind of emptiness. It's a new level of pain. There are parts of your heart that hurt that you didn't even know existed.

When you see a commercial that you and your dad made fun of together. When you hear a song that was in your dad's favorite movie. When the apartment next door is silent, and truly empty.

I look in the mirror and stare at myself. How do I face all these people that are coming to tell me how sorry they are, when I just want to hide myself away and get this over with?

For the first time, I'm grateful that Chuck and my aunt have taken care of everything. I know that if I had to, I could do it—sit down and make all the decisions that need to be made. But it's a huge weight off my shoulders, knowing it's already been done.

"Billie?" I hear Anne's soft voice from the living room. "Are you ready, or do you need a little more time?"

I take one last look at myself and leave the bathroom. "I'm ready," I say.

I slip into my coat and grab my little black clutch. Anne, who's already got her coat on, slips her arm through mine and guides me out.

After locking the door behind us, I lean on my cousin all the way out to the car.

"My mom's meeting us at the funeral home," she says. "She'll have lunch ready, if you're hungry."

I nod, knowing I couldn't eat a thing. "That's nice of her," I say out of obligation. I get into the passenger side of my car. Anne's driving.

I stare out the window all the way there, and I'm thankful that Anne is understanding enough to give me my space and not try to make me talk.

When we pull up to the funeral home, my heart drops. It feels so final. I climb out of the car and face the place where I will officially say goodbye to my father.

I pray for strength and comfort, then I turn to my cousin.

"Let's go."

* * *

The day drags on in a foggy blur. Friends, family, and acquaintances of my dad are all here to show their support. I've been hugged, cried on, pitied, and given advice. The overwhelming smell of flowers turns my stomach. Perhaps it's because I haven't eaten a thing. Or maybe it's because every

Chapter 25

flower reminds me that this is my father's viewing and funeral.

I need some air. I push through the doors of the room and ignore the people standing around, giving me pitying glances. I find the nearest exit and open it, breathing in the cold November air like I've been underwater and have just come to the surface.

Don't you dare have a panic attack right now, Billie! You still have hours to go before this is over.

I find a bench near the parking lot and see that it's unoccupied, so I make my way to it and sit. It's cold, and I didn't stop to grab my coat. But I don't care. The frigid air is a reminder to me that I'm here. That I can feel. That I'm still alive.

I feel a warm hand on my shoulder and look up.

"Prescott," I say, standing.

I can't stop the tears when he takes me in his arms and whispers, "I'm so sorry."

He holds on to me for a moment and I stand there, soaking in his warmth.

"It's too hard," I sob.

"I know," he says, gently squeezing me. "I know."

He loosens his hold and I step back. "Thank you for coming."

"Of course," he says, looking into my eyes. "I didn't know him for long, but your dad was a great man, Billie."

I nod. "Yeah," I whisper.

He puts his arm around my shoulder. "Let's get you inside," he says.

I numbly walk with him back to the room where my father is laid.

As I step through the doorway, I spot Mrs. Joy and Mr. Anderson, and the tears start all over again. Prescott steps away to give me a moment to speak to them.

Mrs. Joy embraces me so tightly, she squeezes the breath right out of me. She pulls back and wipes her own eyes.

"Darn it," she says. "Wouldn't you know, that man found his way right into my heart from day one. And I enjoyed every day I spent with him after that." She wipes her face again. "Thank you, Billie, for sharing your father with me. It was a pleasure to know him."

I hug her again and thank her. She seems to know exactly the right thing to say.

I turn to Mr. Anderson. "Thank you for coming, sir," I say.

He says nothing but reaches out and grabs my hand. Then he gently pulls me toward him and hugs me. The gesture is so intimate, and there are so many people around us that under any other circumstance I'd be embarrassed. But I'm not. It's comforting in a way that words can't describe. I cling to him and cry. He holds me and lets me.

And there, in his embrace, I feel like I just might be able to make it through this day.

Chapter 26

I sit on my couch, holding my coffee. It's been cold for a while, but I don't care. I'm staring out the window. It's quiet.

I can't say that I've hated the time alone, but I will say that sometimes the echoes of my own thoughts ring in my head like a gong. The urge to go next door, walk inside, and see my father sitting on his couch covered in his tattered afghan is nearly overwhelming.

I reach for the ugly afghan that's now on the back of my own couch. I clutch it to my chest and breathe in my dad's scent. It's oddly comforting.

I feel my phone vibrate next to me and see that Anne is wanting to video chat. I hit *ignore* and continue staring out the window.

Lord, help me through today.

Suddenly, I remember a verse from Psalms I memorized when I was a child. *"My comfort in my suffering is this: Your promise preserves my life."*

I know that whatever changes happen in my life, whatever season I go through, no matter what I gain or what I lose, one thing will never change: God's promises and love for me.

This is on my mind as I slip into a much-needed sleep, lying on the couch and clutching my dad's blanket.

* * *

I wake up around 5:20 am. I climb off the couch and head to the bathroom. When I'm finished, I put on a pot of coffee and curl back up on the couch.

I listen to the gurgling sound of the brewing coffee and think about the hours ahead of me. I want nothing more than to hide in my apartment the rest of the day, the rest of the week—the rest of the *month*, for that matter. But I know that it's not an option.

Maybe I should go to work today. It's been nearly a week since the funeral. Mr. Anderson told me to take as much time as I need, but I think it's time to get up and out of the house.

After drinking my first cup of coffee, I jump in the shower.

I'm ready for work before I actually need to leave, but before I head out the door, I stop. I'm used to leaving my apartment a few minutes early so I can stop by my dad's on the way. This feels too weird. Just getting ready and going.

"I miss you, Dad," I whisper, then I lock myself out.

I see Chuck in the hallway; he walks over and gives my shoulders a squeeze.

"Morning, Billie," he says. "How are you doing?"

Chuck is fifty-two, tall, has salt-and-pepper hair, and is quite handsome.

"I'm alright," I say truthfully. "It's hard, but…" I don't finish. He knows.

He pats my shoulder and looks at me. "If there is *anything* you need, Billie…"

I smile. "I know, Chuck, and I appreciate that. You have already done so much, I can't begin to thank you."

"No thanks needed. Your dad was my best friend."

I fight tears as I nod. "He loved you," I say.

Chuck smiles and wishes me a good day. I walk to my car, wondering when this emotional fog will end.

***

When I walk into Mr. Anderson's foyer at around 7:50, I nearly run into Mrs. Joy, who's taking off her coat and hanging it in the front closet.

"Billie!" she says, surprised. "Oh, it's good to see you!" She hugs me fiercely.

Chapter 26

I squeeze her back. "Mrs. Joy. Same. It's good to be back."

She steps back and I see concern filling her face. "Are you sure you're ready?"

I nod. "Yeah. I can't stand sitting alone in my apartment one more day."

"Oh, honey." She hugs me again. "What are you doing Thursday?"

"Thursday?"

She frowns. "Thanksgiving."

"Oh my gosh." I put my palm to my forehead. "I forgot about Thanksgiving." Although, a truer statement might be, *I put the holidays out of my mind because it will be too hard.*

"Billie. Come here Thursday. Please. I'm cooking for Merrick and I've invited Chuck. I want you to come, as well."

"Chuck?" I say, my brow raised.

She laughs. "Of course. He and I got to know one another these past few weeks, and, well, I won't have him sitting home alone on Thanksgiving, either."

I laugh. "That's awesome, Mrs. Joy."

She actually blushes. "Oh, go on."

I sigh. "Alright. I'll come. What can I bring?"

"Any special dishes you make?"

"Hmmm. I make a great sweet potato casserole."

"Perfect. Be here at noon."

I start to head toward the stairs, and I stop. "Thank you," I say.

She smiles and nods.

When I get to the top of the steps, I pause in front of the door to the office. The last time I saw my boss, he was hugging me goodbye after the funeral. I'm not sure if I'll get that Mr. Anderson today, or the all-business, no-time-for-fun Mr. Anderson. I push open the door, ready for either one.

When I enter, he stands to his feet. "Billie," he says. Then he quickly corrects himself with, "Miss Sterling."

I laugh. "Billie is fine, sir. And good morning."

He steps around his desk to meet me at the door as I hang my coat on the rack.

"Are you sure you're ready to come back?" he asks. "How are you?"

I turn and look up at him. The concern in his face makes my heart flutter. It's good to be back in the office with him. I didn't realize how much I've missed him until now. Standing here, looking up at him and remembering his support at the funeral makes me want to throw my arms around him.

The funny thing is, it looks as if he wants to do the same.

We stand there, both of us looking at each other, but neither of us knowing what to do. Finally, I clear my throat. "I'd better get started for the day. You've probably fallen way behind without me here," I tease.

"Miss Sterling," he starts in a stern voice, but something tells me it's a front. "I have worked without an assistant for four years, and I've done just fine without one this past week."

I laugh. "Sure. I'll tell you how 'fine' you've been when I catch up on the messages, mail, phone calls, and all that other little stuff."

He turns to walk to his desk, and I can't see his face. Not that he's easy to read, I remind myself.

"Have you made the coffee?" I ask.

"Yes."

"Okay. I'll go down in a few and make our cups."

I get to my own desk and sit. I can't believe how good it feels just to be out of my apartment today. I don't feel quite as numb. I listen to the voicemail messages and write down a few things for Mr. Anderson.

Then I go make our mugs of coffee.

I like my routine here. There's something comforting about coming into this home, having coffee, seeing Mrs. Joy, and sitting all day near my boss. Things have changed dramatically in my life, and the fact that this piece of my life hasn't changed is nice.

When I get back upstairs, I set Mr. Anderson's coffee down to his right and turn to walk away, when I hear a quiet, "Thank you."

I stop and look at him, but he doesn't look away from his computer screen. "You're welcome," I say, smiling.

When I sit at my desk, I think about how cold Mr. Anderson was to me that first day when I came in for an interview. He's so different now. What if

Chapter 26

I had let his indifference affect me to the point of quitting my job? I'd never have gotten to see this change.

"Miss Sterling."

His voice interrupts my thoughts and I swivel in my chair to face him. "Yes, sir?"

"Are you, uh, *prepared* for the ball?"

"Prepared?" I ask, and I feel a tiny thrill when I remember I'm going with him. "Um, yes?"

"I should be more specific," he says, and his tone is one of discussing business. "Do you have a dress?"

I blink. In all the planning, I've forgotten that I need a dress. "Not yet," I say quietly.

He nods. "I'm adding a bonus to your salary for a dress." He turns, facing his computer again.

Um.

I say nothing as I turn to my own laptop and sip my coffee. I can't help but wonder if his generosity and sudden niceness are because of my father's death. I swallow. *Does he feel sorry for me?*

I feel that weird sinking feeling in the pit of my stomach. I feel like a fool. I should've known. This isn't my boss developing feelings. This is... *pity*.

I feel my face burn as I stare at my screen. Suddenly, I feel bold.

"You don't have to do that, sir."

He turns to look at me. "I told you that I don't do anything I don't want to do."

"I know," I say. "I just... I don't need it."

Now he turns to fully face me. "Yes, you do," he says matter-of-factly.

I stand and walk to his desk. "Why are you doing this?" My voice sounds more than a little irritated.

It doesn't faze my boss a bit as he looks me in the eye and says, "You need my help, that's why."

"Ugh!" I throw my hands in the air. "I don't *need* you to feel sorry for me."

"Is that what you think I'm doing?"

"I *know* you are."

He stands now, coming close to me. "Miss Sterling," he begins in a low voice that holds a hint of warning. "If you ever stopped assuming things, we may actually get somewhere in this re—" he stops, and his face is suddenly stone.

Oh. My. Gosh. Was he going to say "relationship"?

We stare at each other for a moment.

"I'm depositing that bonus with this Friday's check," he finally says. His tone dares me to argue.

Even though my throat is suddenly dry, I manage to get out a quiet, "Okay," before making my way back to my desk.

I mentally scold myself as I sit. *Billie Alexandra! Why do you turn into a puddle every time he talks to you, and why on earth do you agree with everything he says? You hate to be bossed around!*

But in my heart, I know that there's more to it than my boss trying to lord over me.

Deep in my heart, I know he's trying to show he cares.

Chapter 27

When I walk into my building that evening, I'm struck again with the intense sadness of not being able to knock on my dad's door. I let myself in my own apartment and just sit at the table, letting my thoughts wander.

Part of me knows that the pain will get better in time, and part of me wants to sit and wallow in my self-pity. I've never felt such a range of emotions at once.

Suddenly, I think about my bonus check that's coming from Mr. Anderson for a dress. The truth is, I could really use it. But thinking that his motives are driven by pity makes it hard to accept.

Maybe I'm wrong. Lord, I hope I'm wrong.

Another thought hits me as I sit here thinking about the dress I need for the ball. I haven't told Prescott that I won't be going with him.

I pull my phone out of my pocket and stare at it for a moment, gathering the courage to call him. I'm hoping he understands. After all, he *does* know I have feelings for my boss. I just don't want to hurt him. Prescott is a great guy. Any girl would be blessed to…

My thoughts are interrupted by my own brilliant idea, and suddenly I'm excited to call my friend.

He answers after two rings.

"Hey."

"Hey, Prescott," I say.

"Billie. How are you doing? Hanging in there?"

I sigh. "Yeah. At least, I'm trying to."

"One day at a time," he reminds me.

"Yes," I say. "I'm trying."

"So, what's up?"

"Well, I kind of called for a reason."

He chuckles. "I figured."

"Listen," I begin. "Plans have sort of changed."

He's quiet.

"I can't go to the ball with you," I say quietly.

"Wow," he says. "Okay."

"Prescott, I'm so sorry. Mr. Anderson asked me to go with him, and I accepted. It was awful for me to break my date with you, I know, but—"

He cuts me off. "Billie. Don't beat yourself up. It's okay."

"Really?" I ask, skeptically.

"Really. I understand. And I'm happy for you. I realize I'm not the guy for you, and I'm okay with it."

Thank you for understanding," I say softly.

"I really do," he says seriously, before his voice takes on a lighthearted tone. "It just stinks that I've got to find another date, and all the good ones are already taken."

I laugh. "Well," I say, "I just may be able to help you with that."

"Oh no," he says.

"Don't be scared," I say, laughing again. "I know someone who would be absolutely *thrilled* to go to a military ball with a Marine."

"Do you, now?" I hear the smile in his voice, and I can tell he's intrigued.

Perfect.

"My cousin Anne is my age, gorgeous, single, and a Christian," I say, laying it all out on the table.

"Waaaaaiiiit," he draws out the word, and I know what's coming next. "So, what's wrong with her?"

"Ha! What's wrong with *you*?" I counter.

Chapter 27

"Fair enough," he laughs.

I get serious. "She's great, Prescott. She and my aunt put their lives on hold to help out with my dad when he was at his worst. She deserves something like this." I pause and then add, "She deserves someone like you."

"That means a lot. Thank you."

"Of course," I say. "Now, do you want her number or not?"

I can just picture him grinning as he says, "Absolutely."

* * *

I'm just setting my Bible aside, getting ready to turn out the lights, when I get a video call from Anne. I laugh, even before I answer. *I knew it.*

Anne is literally the only person that I will answer on video chat lying in bed with my hair a mess. Besides, I'm way too excited to ignore *this* call.

I hit the *answer* button, and before I can even say a word, Anne is squealing.

"You are the *best* cousin slash best friend in the *world!*"

I grin and shrug. "I try."

"I'm seriously in shock right now," she nearly screams, and once again I turn the volume down to save my ears.

"I knew you would be," I say, laughing.

"That you thought of me for this is the sweetest thing you have ever done, Billie." Then immediately she switches subjects and says, "You didn't tell me about going to the ball with Merrick Anderson, by the way!"

I shrug again. "There was a lot going on."

"Yeah. That's why you're forgiven."

"Oh, *thank* you," I say, rolling my eyes.

She laughs. "Billie, he sounds so cute over the phone. Tell me everything about him," she demands.

"Did you forget I haven't known him that long?"

"Well, you've known him what, like one hundred percent longer than I have?"

I shake my head at her math. "It's been less than two months."

"Two months is *plenty* of time to get to know a person. Now remind me again, does he play tennis?"

"Anne!" I jokingly scold her.

"Just kidding, just kidding."

We spend the next half hour chatting about Prescott. She asks me every question she can think of, and I answer to the best of my knowledge.

Finally, I say, "That's about all I can tell you, Anne. The rest you'll have to find out for yourself."

"But the ball is so far away!"

"So, ask him if he'd like to get together beforehand."

She's still, and I can almost see the wheels turning in her blond head. "Hmm. Not a bad idea."

"Of course not," I say. "When have I ever had a bad idea?"

Too quickly, she answers, "When we stole that Kmart shopping cart and took turns pushing each other around the neighborhood."

We both burst into laughter thinking about our eighth-grade shenanigans.

"I wouldn't use that as a conversation starter on your first date," I say.

"What do you mean? That's the *perfect* first date story!"

After another fit of laughter, I get serious.

"Thank you, Anne. I needed this."

She smiles. "You're doing great, you know."

I feel my eyes burn and hate how quickly my emotions do an about-face.

"I don't *feel* like I am," I say, honestly.

"It's gonna take some time, Bill," she tells me.

I nod. "I know," I whisper. I wipe at my cheek. "I'd better go. I'm already back to work, so that means up and at 'em early tomorrow."

"Hey," she says. "Thanks again."

"No problem," I say, waving my hand.

"Let's go dress shopping together!"

"We totally can," I say, thinking about my bonus coming. "Black Friday?"

Her eyes light up. "Are you sure you're up for *that*?"

"If I fill my thermos with coffee and pray before we go."

She laughs. "Perfect. Friday it is, then."

We end the call, and I fall asleep smiling.

Chapter 27

* * *

I'm just hanging up the phone the next day when Mrs. Joy knocks on the office door, then pops her head in.

"Mr. Anderson," she says in her most business-like voice, and I know someone's out in the hall with her. "Mr. Wakefield is here to see you."

"Send him in."

A second later, Prescott walks through the door. He flashes a brilliant smile at me before walking to Mr. Anderson's desk and shaking his hand.

"Merrick."

"Prescott."

And that's the extent of the hellos. I smile and shake my head, then turn to my laptop. *Men.*

"Good morning, Billie," I hear Prescott say.

I look up at him and grin. "Good afternoon, you mean."

He glances at his watch. "So it is. Have you talked to your cousin?"

I laugh. "You know I have."

"I think I remember seeing someone that could've been her at the funeral," he says thoughtfully. "But there were so many people there, I'm not sure."

"I'm so sorry I didn't get to introduce you," I say.

"No worries. You had a lot on your mind."

"*I* have a lot on my *agenda*," Mr. Anderson interjects. "Could you finish this conversation later?"

"Of course, sir," I say, smiling sweetly. Then I look at Prescott and roll my eyes.

He laughs, and my boss scowls.

Then Prescott says something that tempts me to crawl under my desk and shrivel up.

"You'd better take care of her at the ball, Merrick, since you stole her from me."

Silence. Stony, icy silence.

I don't even dare a look in Mr. Anderson's direction. I just sit at my desk, my face burning.

It's getting unbearably awkward when Prescott starts laughing. "You've *got* to lighten up, Merrick. I'm kidding."

I let out a breath and feel the sudden urge to slap my new friend. I finally chance a look in my employer's direction. His face looks chiseled from granite. He obviously didn't find the comment funny.

Prescott shakes his head, still laughing. "Let's go over this stuff," he says, and pushes a binder toward Mr. Anderson.

I turn back to my desk, thinking of all the creative ways to give Prescott a piece of my mind later.

***

It's the end of the day. Prescott is gone, and Mrs. Joy left early today to start shopping for Thanksgiving, so it's just me and my boss now. I'm straightening my desk and making sure I've finished everything on my agenda.

Suddenly, I look up from my desk to find Mr. Anderson standing there.

"Did you need something before I leave?"

"No."

"Oh. Okay." I go back to straightening up.

"Do you wish you hadn't said yes to me, and that you were still going with him?"

I stop what I'm doing and turn to him. "No. Not at all."

He nods, and I see a brief flash of relief across his face.

"And I don't really think Prescott is upset, either."

"I don't care what he thinks."

"Oh, right," I say, quickly.

"I just don't want you to go with me, but wish you were there with him."

I shake my head. "Not going to happen."

He looks at me for a moment, and I feel a little self-conscious under his gaze. I nervously tuck my hair behind my ear and reach for my purse.

"Are you going home?"

I look at the clock. It's after five. "Um, yeah, I was," I say. "But if you need

Chapter 27

me for something, I can stay."

"No," he says, "I don't need you to stay. I guess what I should've asked is if you have plans or if you're just going home."

I swallow a lump forming in my throat. *My dad is gone. No plans whatsoever.* But I just shake my head. "I'm going home," I say. "No plans."

"Have dinner with me."

It's a command, not a question.

"F-for work?" I ask quietly.

He steps toward me, and once again, I tip my head back to look at him as he gets closer.

"No, Billie," he says. "Not for work."

Oh.

"Okay," I whisper.

He nods and walks over to the rack to get my coat. He comes back and holds it up for me.

As I slip my arms in, he says, "I was thinking of Antonio's. Are you in the mood for Italian?"

"Anything is fine with me," I say, but inwardly I cringe at the thought of their prices.

I follow him out the door and to his car.

We're driving in silence when he suddenly says, "You don't have to order soup and salad, you know."

I turn to look at him, and I'm glad that it's dark enough that he can't see me blush. "I like soup and salad," I say softly.

"I understand, and soup and salad are fine for lunch. But this is dinner, and I want you to order what looks good to you, regardless of price."

I'm a bit embarrassed. Am I that transparent?

"Alright," I agree.

He nods, apparently satisfied with my answer.

I turn to look out the window, and it hits me.

I'm on a *date* with Mr. Anderson.

Chapter 28

We walk into Antonio's and I'm glad I at least wore a skirt to work today. Everyone seems so formal. We're dressed in business attire, but one glance at my boss tells me he couldn't care less what others think. He asks for a booth, and the host seems excited to seat us. I wonder if he recognizes Mr. Anderson.

The place is crowded—much more so than when we were here for lunch—and as Mr. Anderson follows the host to the table, I get cut off by a large party leaving, and I lose him.

Suddenly, I feel a warm hand grab mine, and I look up to see my boss tugging me along.

He didn't leave me. My heart flutters a bit at the thoughtful gesture.

I follow him to our booth, and after the host takes our coats, I slide in.

Suddenly I feel shy and a little unsure of myself. I've been to restaurants with him more than a few times now, but it was always to discuss business, or stopping on our way somewhere.

This is different, though.

This is a *date*.

I run my palms over my skirt under the table, and I feel a little like I did when I walked into Mr. Anderson's office that day for the interview. My hands are sweaty, a sure sign of my nerves.

Get it under control, Billie! I order myself.

Chapter 28

The waiter fills our water glasses, then leaves us to look over the menu. I try to keep my eyes from going wide at the prices. *And I thought lunch was expensive!*

"What looks good to you?" I ask, trying to sound casual. If I know what he's ordering, I'll stay around that price range.

Mr. Anderson gently sets his menu down and looks me in the eyes. "What looks good to *you*, Billie?"

I manage to keep from swooning. After hearing "Miss Sterling" a hundred times a day, I love the sound of him saying my first name.

"Um, I'm not sure," I say.

"Billie. I want you to look over this menu and order what you want. Period." He lifts the menu back up to cover his face, but I hear him add, "And *you* are ordering first, so you can't just say you'll have what I'm having."

Darn.

I pick up my menu and try to focus on the food, not the prices. My eyes land on a dish that looks delicious. My mouth waters, and I know it's what I want. It's a salmon dish with artichokes and a lemon garlic sauce.

I set my menu down, and Mr. Anderson does too. In a few seconds, the waiter is back at our table for our orders. I order the salmon, and Mr. Anderson orders a beef tenderloin dish with fresh vegetables. The waiter takes our menus and assures us our food will be up momentarily.

"Thank you for taking me to dinner, sir," I begin.

"Billie."

"Yes?" I say softly.

"While we're here, will you call me Merrick?"

I laugh a little. "I don't know if I can. It's… weird."

I see the corner of his mouth tip up ever so slightly. "It is, I guess," he says. "I've grown quite fond of hearing 'sir' day after day."

I laugh again and set my napkin on my lap, for no other reason than needing to do something with my hands. I wish this weren't so awkward.

"And about taking you to dinner," he says.

I look up at him.

"It's my pleasure."

My heart works overtime after hearing those words. I'm fairly certain my boss can hear it trying to pound out of my chest.

My boss. How can I think of him as anything else?

But I do.

I'm hopelessly attracted to him and my feelings grow stronger every day that I'm around him. Sitting across from him now—not as his employee, but his date—has me wondering desperately if he could feel even a little the way I do.

"Merrick," I say, smiling, then I repeat it. "Merrick. Yeah, I could get used to that."

"So could I."

Oh, boy. My mouth goes dry and I try to swallow. I reach for my water and take a sip too quickly, spilling it on myself. I grab my napkin and frantically blot at the droplets all over my maroon dress shirt. I feel my face burning, and know it's probably bright red.

I see him reach across the table, and before I can react, he grabs my hand. I look up at him, miserably embarrassed.

"Billie," he says, his voice low. "I'm sorry If I've made you uncomfortable around me."

I just stare at him, so he continues.

"I wasn't exactly friendly to you when you first started working for me."

I laugh now. *"That's* an understatement."

He's still serious. "But you stayed."

"I stayed," I whisper.

"Why?"

This conversation is getting intense, so I try to lighten the mood by shrugging and saying, "The money."

Our food arrives at that moment, and letting go of my hand, my boss shocks me once more.

"Will you pray, Billie?"

"Of course," I say. We both bow our heads. "Thank You, Father, for this wonderful food before us. Thank You for Your blessings that we surely don't deserve." I pause, then pray, "Thank You for Merrick and his generous heart.

Chapter 28

And thank You that no matter how far we've drifted, we're always only one step from being home. Amen."

When I look up, Mr. Anderson is looking at me—not with his usual cold eyes, but with eyes filled with hope.

I smile at him.

He quickly looks down at his food and begins to eat.

* * *

Tonight, I basically float into my apartment.

Dinner was great.

The conversation was even better.

And my boss is more than I imagined him to be.

All these weeks I came in day after day, feeling as though I'd never be able to see past the stony exterior. Tonight, however, I can imagine that tough shell cracking, and pieces falling to the ground. There is definitely a softer man inside.

I say a quick prayer of thanks, grateful that God is faithful to do what He's promised. All those prayers I've sent up for Merrick Anderson, and I've always just felt that God was reminding me to be patient; He had it all under control.

I send a text to Anne, asking if she's still awake.

Eight seconds later, my phone rings.

I answer, laughing. "What took you so long?"

"Aaaaaah! I have a date!"

"Aaaaaah!" I squeal back. "I just had a date!"

"What?!"

"You do??"

We laugh at our simultaneous answers.

"You first," I say.

"So, I called Prescott, and I casually mentioned that we should grab a coffee or something before the ball, you know, just to get to know each other. He said that it sounded like an excellent idea, and we're going out Friday night!

Eeeeek!"

"Anne, I'm so excited for you! You are going to have a great time. He's amazing."

"I'd like to say that I'm sorry it didn't work out between you two, but I'm really not sorry at all," she says, and I laugh.

"It's okay," I say. "I'm not sorry, either. Especially because I just got back from dinner with *Merrick*." I say his first name slowly, hoping she notices my lack of formality.

"Oh. My. Word. You should've gone first!"

"Anne, it was incredible. He's nothing like what he seemed in the beginning."

"You really like him."

"I *really* do."

"I'm happy for us," she says.

"Me too," I say grinning.

We're both quiet for a moment, then she says, "Your dad would've been really happy, too, you know."

"I know. He liked Merrick. A lot."

"At least you know you have his blessing."

"Yeah," I say quietly, and I know it's true.

Anne sighs and tells me she'd better go. She and my aunt are headed down to Ohio to spend Thanksgiving with Anne's grandparents on her father's side.

"Are you sure you'll be up to Black Friday shopping?" I ask.

"Absolutely," she says. "We'll be back home by ten at the latest. Plenty of time for me to get a few hours of sleep."

"Have a safe trip, and a good Thanksgiving," I say.

"You too, Bill."

* * *

It's Wednesday, and I walk into the office unsure. Do I go back to calling him "sir"? *Of course you do, Billie; this is your job!* I mentally scold myself.

Chapter 28

When I step in and see him already sitting at his desk, my heart skips as I remember our date the night before.

He stops typing and looks up at me. Then he smiles.

Oh, how I love that smile.

"Good morning," he says, and because it's early, his voice is still low and gravelly.

I can't help but smile back as I say good morning.

He goes back to his typing and I hang my coat up. I set my purse in the drawer and then walk back to the door.

He looks up and I say, "Be right back. Coffee."

He nods, and I slip through the door and head downstairs.

Mrs. Joy, wearing a freshly cleaned apron, is in the kitchen. There's food everywhere.

I laugh. "You don't play around when it comes to Thanksgiving dinner, do you?"

"Billie!" she says, and when she looks up, I see flour on her chin. "I just thought I'd get a head start."

"Mrs. Joy," I begin, "I hope it's alright for me to ask, what about your family? Don't you see them on Thanksgiving?"

She nods and starts rolling her pie crust. "I do," she says. "Every other year. This year, my kids spend it with their in-laws."

"Oh, that's nice. And I'm sure Mr. Anderson doesn't mind the company."

"Not at all," she says. "That man loves to eat."

I laugh. "I've noticed. Especially since…" I let my voice trail off, not knowing how to say it.

She stops rolling and her head snaps up. "Since what?"

I grin and step close to her, whispering, "Since we went out for dinner last night. Together."

Her eyes grow wide and she whispers back, "Like a date?"

I nod. "*Definitely* a date."

She covers her mouth with her hand and I've never seen her look so pleased. "Oh, Billie. You've just made my day."

I giggle and hug her.

"I can't wait for tomorrow," she says.

"Me neither," I say.

I realize at this moment that this is the first time since my dad passed that I'm truly looking forward to something.

Chapter 29

I daydream as I make my sweet potato casserole. I think about getting up early, preparing for dinner, and watching America's Thanksgiving Parade with my dad. We always said we'd go down to Detroit and be part of it one year, but we never got the chance.

I take a sip of my coffee and fight tears. *How long will every memory make me cry?* I just want to get to the point where I can think of my dad and just smile. I shake myself and remember that I've got a great day ahead of me. I stick my casserole in the oven and jump into the shower.

I want to look nice but also be comfortable. I pull on some cute leggings with colored leaves on them and a loose, burnt-orange dress shirt that goes nearly to my knees. After tying a belt around my middle, I pull my hair to the side and loosely braid it so that it falls over my shoulder. Checking the mirror, I'm satisfied with my look.

Once I'm ready, I glance at the clock. I've got time. I sit on the couch and flip open my Bible while waiting for the ding of the oven timer.

"This is for you, Dad," I say to my empty apartment. Then I read out loud. "'Oh, that men would give thanks to the Lord for His great love and for the wonderful things He has done for them. For He satisfies the thirsty and fills the hungry with good things.' Psalm 107:8-9."

I sigh and close my Bible. Dad and I read those verses every Thanksgiving.

I hear the ding of the oven and go to the kitchen to pull my casserole out.

After placing it carefully into the insulated carrier, I put on my coat, grab my things, and head out the door.

***

On the way there I try not to think about my dad not being with me. And knowing him as I did, I'm sure he'd want me to have a great time and enjoy my day. It's just hard. I miss him terribly.

Not wanting to arrive at Mr. Anderson's home with red-rimmed eyes, I flip on the radio for a distraction. It works, and in no time, I'm singing along with the music.

As I pull into the driveway I see that Mrs. Joy has set out an adorable display of pumpkins and friendly scarecrows. How do I know it was Mrs. Joy, you may ask? Well, we know it wasn't my boss, now, don't we?

I park and step out of my car, grabbing my casserole and checking my appearance one last time in the reflection of the window. I take a deep breath and head inside.

If the smells that hit me when I walk through the door are any indicator of how the food is going to taste, I know I'm in for a treat. Mrs. Joy has obviously been working night and day to make this feast happen. Suddenly, I feel a little self-conscious about my small casserole I brought to contribute.

Fortunately, my fears are put to rest when Mrs. Joy greets me by taking my dish and thanking me for making it. She leans down and breathes deeply, smiling and telling me how wonderful it smells.

"Thanks," I say. "So does this house! You must've worked so hard."

She waves dismissively and says, "Oh, it was nothing. I love to do it. Now come on in and relax—you're not an employee today. You're family."

I can't help but tear up at her words. "Thank you," I say softly, taking off my coat.

I make my way into the living room where I hear the TV. Mr. Anderson is sitting in the exact spot I put him when he was sick. Only this time, he doesn't look sleepy or feverish. He looks incredible.

He's wearing dark jeans and a brown and tan sweater that's the perfect

Chapter 29

shape and fit for him. He looks relaxed and… *happy.*

"Billie," he says when he spots me. He stands and smiles at me.

Nope. Still not tired of that smile.

"Please, sit down," he says, and unless my mind is playing tricks on me, I'd say he's nervous. "I'll be right back." He heads to the kitchen.

I take a seat on the couch where he's sitting, but I leave an entire cushion between us. I don't want to make him feel weird.

Or maybe I feel weird.

Billie, stop! You're acting like a high schooler. This is just a normal holiday with normal people.

Except it's anything but normal, and you're spending it with your hot boss.

My face burns at my own thoughts and I bury my face in my hands. I nearly start laughing. Why am I so nervous?

"Here we go."

I look up and instantly forget about my thoughts. Mr. Anderson—or Merrick, I guess I should be calling him today—is standing there with a coffee cup in his hand. He holds it out to me.

"Just cream, right?"

"Right," I say. "How did you know?"

The side of his mouth tips up. "Margaret knows *everything*."

I take the cup and he sits down in his previous spot.

"Thank you," I say. "That was sweet of you."

He nods. "You bring me coffee every day. I thought I'd return the favor."

I take a sip. Pumpkin spice. I smile. "It's very good."

He looks proud and I almost laugh.

"Do you like football?" he asks, gesturing to the TV.

I see that the Lions pre-game show is on, and I shrug. "I'm not a mega fan, but I like to watch sometimes." I leave out the part where my dad and I watched the Lions play every Thanksgiving.

"Great," he says.

"Great," I echo, taking a sip of my coffee. I roll my eyes at my lame response. *It's just like any Monday morning, Billie. Only you're not answering phones. You can totally do this.*

Mrs. Joy chooses that moment to bring us a tray of crackers, summer sausage, and cheese. Her timing is impeccable. I gratefully take a piece of each and thank her.

"The food will be ready around halftime," she says.

"Perfect," my boss answers.

We hear a knock on the door and Mrs. Joy says, "There's Chuck. I hope he remembered the pumpkin pie."

As she walks to the door, I glance at the man sitting next to me. "It's kind of cool, Chuck coming here today."

He nods.

A moment later, Chuck is sitting in the living room with us as the national anthem begins.

The game starts off well enough, with Detroit taking an early lead over the Packers. But it's the Lions—that could change at any moment. I decide to sit back and try to enjoy the game, no matter the outcome.

We're still winning at halftime, so the guys are in a great mood as Mrs. Joy calls us for dinner.

We gather at the table and I'm struck with a warmth in my chest. This feels like family. Not having my father with me this Thanksgiving still hurts—but being here today makes it bearable.

Mrs. Joy holds out the carving knife. "Merrick, would you do the honors?"

Merrick stands and gestures to me. "I'd like Billie to say the blessing first."

"I'd be honored," I say, truthfully.

But as I start to pray, I get a bit choked up, stumbling over my words. I'm thanking the Lord for friends and family, but the absence of my father is ever-looming. I push through the tears and manage to finish the prayer.

When I look up, Mrs. Joy is smiling tearfully. "That was just beautiful, Billie."

I nod in thanks, not wanting to speak for fear of my voice wobbling.

Merrick looks at me and says nothing. I don't mind, though, because it's not one of his usual icy stares.

In fact, it's very warm. I blush and look away.

Dinner is incredible. I haven't had much of Mrs. Joy's cooking, but I

Chapter 29

believe my boss when he tells her that she's outdone herself. As for Chuck, he just can't stop giving her compliments. Mrs. Joy eats it up, waving her hand like she does, pretending it was nothing.

Everyone loves my casserole. Mrs. Joy insists on having the recipe. I laugh and tell her that I'll write it down before I leave.

All in all, it's a great time. And I can truly say that today, my grief was lessened just a bit.

* * *

I've never seen my boss so excited. About anything. But it's the fourth quarter at the two-minute warning and the Lions are in the lead, 24-14.

Seeing him jump off the couch and yell at the TV every few minutes is highly entertaining. This is a side of Merrick Anderson I never thought I'd see. I don't think I really even believed it existed.

But here he is, high-fiving Chuck and cheering the team on through the TV as if they can hear him. And when the game finally ends, I get the surprise of my life when he pulls me off the couch and bear-hugs me, lifting me off the floor.

I'm laughing when he sets me down, then quickly become serious when I realize he's still holding me.

Looking down at me, he says, "You must be my good-luck charm."

I blush as my heart pounds. "Maybe," I whisper.

He lets me go and I sit back down, heart still thumping.

Merrick sits next to me. I've been to lunch and dinner with him several times now, but this feels more intimate than those times. I sit still, a little worried I'll do something embarrassing.

You've got to relax, Billie.

It's just that this changing dynamic between us has me on edge. I'm excited, nervous, and scared all at once. My dad isn't here to talk to and I'm trying to sort my feelings.

I remind myself that I've left this in God's hands and I need to leave it there, trusting that He'll take care of it all—my feelings, Merrick's feelings, this budding relationship. I sigh. *Is this a relationship?*

Merrick turns to me, a slight scowl on his face. "Everything alright?"

I realize that my thoughts must be affecting my countenance and I force a smile. "I'm fine," I say.

He nods, and weirdly, the gesture is comforting.

Chuck gets up to join Mrs. Joy in the kitchen. I tried to help her with cleanup, but she insisted I stay with Merrick and finish the game. Now it's just the two of us sitting here.

"So," he begins, adjusting himself on the couch to face me. "Have you gotten your dress?"

I shake my head. "Going tomorrow with Anne."

His eyes widen. "You're going to tackle the Black Friday crowd?"

I laugh. "Absolutely. That's what coffee's for. And prayer," I add.

He stares at me intently for a moment until I ask what he's thinking.

"Just how beautiful you'd look in a blue dress," he says.

Um.

I swallow. *Who is this charmer and what has he done with my boss?*

"Uh, thanks," I say. "I'm not sure what I'm getting yet. I've got to find something that I can make work for the 1910s theme."

"You'll look great," he says, and my face heats at the look in his eye.

I stand. "I'm going to grab some coffee," I say, needing a minute to myself. I head into the kitchen.

When I walk in, I see Chuck leaning over Mrs. Joy, both of them laughing about something. They look adorable together and I'm happy for them.

I sigh, pouring my fresh cup of coffee.

Everything is changing and I'm not sure how I feel about it all. I pray that God keeps my heart safely in His hands.

Chapter 30

"This is insane!" I scan the crowd of people.

Anne laughs, which makes me laugh.

"It's all part of the experience," she says. "Besides, we've got our coffee—we'll be fine."

It's 4:40 am and we're in a popular formal dress shop. The line to the register is almost to the door.

I sigh. "I hope I find a dress that's worth standing in this line."

"You will," says Anne, pure delight in her eyes. "I just know it."

We separate for a few, Anne looking in one area and me in another. After a few moments, I hear Anne gasp and I know she's found something.

"Look," she breathes. "Isn't it *gorgeous*?"

She holds up a deep red off-the-shoulder gown.

"It is," I agree. "Very Christmassy. It's perfect for you."

"I'm going to try it on."

I'm surprised she's not jumping up and down.

I turn to my rack and keep looking. Close by, a lady and her teenage daughter are obviously having a blast finding Christmas dresses. I feel a sudden twinge of jealousy when I think of all those moments I never got to experience. But I'm happy for the girl and her mom. I just hope they realize what they have.

When I go back to my shopping, I hear Anne call my name. Trying not to trample anyone, I make my way over to the dressing room. Anne pops her head out, smiling.

"Let me see," I say.

She steps out and I suck in my breath. "Anne. That is stunning."

She nods excitedly. "I still may try on a few more for fun." She shrugs. "But I'm pretty confident that this is the one."

"It looks amazing on you."

She beams. "Thanks."

She steps back into the dressing room and I go back to looking for my dress. I see a clearance rack and head that way. Then I remember my bonus. *You don't need to go cheap this time, Billie.* I recall my shock when I called my automated banking number and learned that I had received a five-hundred-dollar bonus. That was enough for shoes and a new purse. Heck, I might even get my hair done professionally.

Anne finds me a moment later, red gown in hand. "Come with me." Grabbing my hand, she pulls me back the way she came, through the sea of people.

"Look what I found."

My eyes fall on the dress she's pointing to and I inhale softly. "Oh my gosh. It's gorgeous."

It's a vintage-style gown with an empire waist, and…

"It's blue."

"You don't like blue?"

I shake my head. "No, I do. It's just that he…"

Anne tips her head, waiting for me to finish.

"Mr. Anderson—Merrick, I mean—suggested I get a blue dress."

Before I can say another word, Anne is pushing me toward the fitting rooms and shoving the blue dress in my hands.

"Get in there. Now."

I laugh. "You are too much." I take the dress from her and close the door behind me.

When I slip it on, it just *feels* right. The color looks great on me, and I can imagine the completed look with the right shoes and hairstyle.

Chapter 30

"Well?" I hear Anne's voice from the other side of the door.

"I love it."

"I knew it."

"You have a great eye for fashion."

"I know."

We both laugh.

I take one more look at myself in the dress, sigh, and switch back into my clothes. Walking out of the dressing room, I see Anne looking through another rack.

She sees me and asks if I'm ready to get in line.

"Yep," I say. "And next stop—shoes."

She grins. "Bring it on."

* * *

Monday morning has my stomach in knots. It's a work day like any other, but I'm just not sure how to act around my boss anymore. I think of the way he held me after the game, the way he smiled at me... even his low, intimate tone when he spoke to me. I blush thinking about it.

Do I go back to calling him sir? At work, is it inappropriate to call him Merrick? *Of course it is, you ninny!* I can't just waltz into the office and say, "Hey, Merrick, what's up?"

I laugh out loud at my own thoughts as I pull into the driveway. After parking, I walk up to the door, determined not to make a fool of myself today. I decide that I'll take my cue from my boss. If he calls me Billie, I'll call him Merrick. Same with the formal names.

When I walk upstairs to the office, however, I'm disappointed. When I say good morning, he only nods. At least it's not a cold nod. He actually smiles and makes me feel like he's happy to see me. But still, he doesn't call me anything.

Darn.

After hanging my coat, I head to my desk. I see a little plastic box on my desk and I pick it up. It's a new oil for my plug-in called Christmas Spirit. I sniff it and close my eyes. It *does* smell like Christmas. I turn and smile at the man responsible.

"Thank you for the new scent."

He stops typing and turns to me. "You're welcome."

He looks so handsome this morning. How can I work with him day after day and not be distracted by his presence?

After placing my personal things in the desk drawer, I head down to make the coffee. I expect to run into Mrs. Joy, but she's nowhere to be seen. I shrug and get started on the coffee.

A few moments later, I'm headed upstairs with two steaming cups. When I set my boss's down, I ask him about Mrs. Joy.

"I gave her the day off." He takes a sip of his coffee. "She had such a long weekend, I told her to stay home and watch all those black and white movies she's so fond of."

"Aw, you're sweet," I say, sipping my own coffee.

His eyebrow raises. "Am I?"

I feel my face grow warm. "Well, I'm sure Mrs. Joy thinks so." I head to my desk.

"There's a lot to be done today. The ball is in two weeks."

"I know, I can't believe it."

"Did you find a dress?"

"I did," I say, smiling.

"Good." He turns back to his computer.

I wait a moment, then say, "I really appreciated the bonus, sir."

He turns back to me. "So, we're back to sir, now?" I see the amusement in his eyes.

I shrug. "I don't know what to call you, now that…"

He stands and walks to my desk, coffee in hand. "Now that what?"

I get a bit flustered trying to find the words. "Well, it's just that you told me to call you Merrick, but that was when we weren't working. It just seems inappropriate to call you by your first name at work. You are, after all, my boss."

He smiles, "I think I have a solution. When it's just the two of us here in

Chapter 30

the office, we'll use Billie and Merrick. If we're meeting with a client or out in public, it's Mr. Anderson and Miss Sterling."

"Okay." I nod. "That sounds good."

Merrick takes a sip of coffee but doesn't immediately walk back to his desk.

"Is there… anything else?" I ask.

"I'm just… glad you're here."

"Oh," I say, softly. "Me too."

"I mean, I'm *really* glad I turned down the first forty interviewees."

I laugh. "You know what they say, the forty-first time's the charm."

He steps closer, then sits on the corner of my desk and looks down at me. "Yeah. It was."

I can't help it—I blush. Him casually sitting on my desk like this is totally… *intimate*.

I swallow and say, "You didn't like me at first."

"Not true."

"Um, I'm pretty sure it *is* true," I laugh.

"I'm sorry if I made you think I didn't like you, Billie."

I shrug in nonchalance, playing with a pen on my desk. "I didn't think you liked anybody."

I expect him to laugh, but he doesn't.

"Your being here…" he begins.

I look up at him.

"It's made me think about a lot of things."

"Really?" I ask, and my voice feels small.

"Really. After Sophia, I… well, I didn't think I'd ever…"

My heart practically beats out of my chest. He's looking at me intently, and I can't tear my eyes from his.

What? You didn't think you'd ever what?

Suddenly, he's leaning forward.

Ohmygosh ohmygosh ohmygosh!

I swallow hard, and I can feel my palms sweating.

Then he stops leaning toward me and stands up.

"We have a lot of work to do." He turns and walks to his desk.

I sit at my own desk for a moment, wondering what just happened. *Was he going to kiss me?*

Merrick sits down and stares at his computer screen.

Frantically, I look for something to do, even though I know I won't be able to concentrate. I find a list of follow-up calls I need to make, confirming details for the ball. Perfect.

For the next hour or so, I busy myself with the phone calls, only speaking to my boss when I have to. I'm not trying to make things more awkward, but I'm not sure what it was that almost happened and I'm afraid I'll say something stupid. You know, like, "Why didn't you kiss me, sir?"

I place my hand over my face, thankful that my boss doesn't have mind-reading abilities.

* * *

It's lunchtime, and I'm hoping I can sneak off and get an hour to myself. But when I grab my jacket and let Merrick know I'm leaving, he stands.

"Wait, Billie. Don't leave for lunch today."

"Um, okay?" I'm a bit confused. What's going on with him?

He reaches for his desk phone and I see him set it to voicemail. Then he comes to stand by me.

"Margaret made pot pies with the leftover food from Thanksgiving." He shrugs, "I figured we can have them for lunch today."

I'm a little relieved that he's not feeling as weird as I am—at least he doesn't seem to be. So I agree and follow him down to the kitchen.

As soon as we get downstairs, however, he turns and takes me into his arms. Before I get the chance to let shock set in, he leans down, his mouth brushing my ear.

"I didn't think this was appropriate to do in the office during work hours," he murmurs.

Then he presses his lips to mine.

Chapter 31

I freeze, excitement thrumming through my chest. *This.* This is what I've been waiting for.

I can't help wrapping my arms around his neck, and he pulls me closer. When he finally ends the kiss, he steps back, taking my hand.

"That was okay?" he asks.

I nod quickly, heart still pounding. "That was okay."

"Good." He turns and leads me into the kitchen.

Merrick heats up the pies like nothing in the world is different, but I'm afraid to eat for fear of choking on my own elation.

I sit on a stool at the island counter, watching him. He gets two plates from the cupboard and sets them in front of me.

"Can I help?"

He shakes his head. "Nah, I got it. Just tell me what you want to drink."

"Do you have iced tea?"

"Yep." He turns to the fridge and pulls out a pitcher. "Margaret puts fresh raspberries in it."

"Yum."

He gets both glasses out and pours us each some tea. He sets mine in front of me and smiles.

I suddenly feel shy and wonder if he's still thinking about the kiss. I know I am.

As if I could think about anything else. I honestly don't know how I'm going to get through the rest of the day.

When the food is warmed, Merrick joins me at the counter to eat. I manage to chew and swallow my pot pie like a sane person—so that's a plus. But I barely taste the food because I can't think of anything except the man sitting next to me.

Oh my gosh, Billie. You are like a lovesick schoolgirl.

We eat in silence, occasionally glancing at each other and smiling. When we're done, Merrick takes our dishes and puts them in the sink.

"Would you mind making some fresh coffee?"

"Not at all," I say, grateful for something to do where I can be alone with my thoughts for a few moments.

He nods and heads out of the kitchen.

I sigh, relaxing for the first time since we came down the stairs.

Breathe, I tell myself, as I get up to make the coffee. *You're gonna make it through this day just fine.*

Knowing my track record for doing stupid things, I hope I can believe myself.

* * *

I think about my dad a lot throughout the rest of the day. I know he liked and approved of Merrick, and I know he'd be happy at what's developing between us.

I'm also sad I won't be able to tell him.

It's a weird thing when grief and happiness share a place in your heart. Every day I wake up longing to see and talk to my father. The pain of loss and emptiness sometimes feels like it's too much to bear. Then I think of coming to work and seeing the man I'm falling hard for, and it brings a joy I can't describe. It's a sweet feeling mixed in with the bitter.

Sitting now at my desk, I must have quite a look on my face, because my boss asks me if I'm alright.

"Yeah," I say softly. "Just missing my dad."

Chapter 31

He nods and says nothing, but I see concern in his eyes. We both go back to work.

We work quietly for the next little while, both of us focused on finishing our tasks. I'm lost in my own thoughts when I suddenly notice Merrick standing by my desk. I look up and smile.

"I had a thought," he says.

"Oh?"

"Yeah. I plan on eating dinner here, alone. You're going home to eat dinner alone. Why not just stay after work and eat dinner together?"

My grin widens. "That's a great idea."

He nods and goes back to his desk.

I figure my cheeks will probably be sore later on account of all this smiling I'm doing, but I don't care. I steal a glance at Merrick one more time before getting back to work.

And one more time I thank God for this bit of sunshine peeking through my season of rain.

* * *

We end up working until almost six—wrapping up all the loose ends, taking care of last-minute changes, returning phone calls. It's apparent that we're both exhausted, and I'm thankful that the work day is finally over.

"So, what's on the menu?" I ask, grabbing my coat and purse, ready to head downstairs.

"Well, uh," Merrick runs his hand through his hair, looking a little sheepish. "I don't really cook, so I was thinking frozen pizza."

I laugh. "Sounds good. Unless…"

He quirks an eyebrow.

"I could look through your fridge and pantry—see what you have to work with?"

"You feel like cooking?"

"I'd cook if I went home."

"Alright. Margaret keeps me pretty well stocked, so let's see what we have."

We head downstairs. I'm starting to feel at home here, and my heart warms at the thought of us cooking together in his kitchen.

When we open the fridge, I see chicken breast, ground beef, and sliced ham.

"There's a few options," I say, turning to the pantry. After opening it, I know what I want to make.

I grab a box of noodles and hold it up. "Spaghetti?"

He nods. "Sounds great to me."

He grabs the pots and pans while I pull out the spices and sauce.

"Do you prefer meat and sauce, or meatballs?"

He shrugs. "Haven't had spaghetti and meatballs in forever. It actually sounds really good."

"Great," I say. "You can help me."

After washing our hands and preheating the oven, I put the ground beef into a bowl and tell him which spices I need. I grab an egg from the fridge and breadcrumbs from the pantry.

After mixing the beef with the other ingredients, I show Merrick how to form the meatballs and arrange them on the pan, ready for the oven.

After a moment, I burst out laughing. His meatballs are horribly misshapen and all different sizes.

He scowls at me. "What?"

"Nothing," I say, trying to keep my laughter under control. "Nothing at all."

He looks down at his work. "You're lying."

This time I can't stop myself from laughing. "I *am* lying. You're terrible at this."

Merrick ends up sitting at the island counter while I finish dinner. I don't mind, though. He's there to talk to me while I finish up, and I'm just enjoying the time together.

Once the spaghetti is ready, I pray and we make our plates. Then he motions for me to follow him into the living room.

"Are you okay with eating in here?"

"Absolutely."

Chapter 31

He sets his plate and tea down on the coffee table and picks up the TV remote. I take a seat on the couch while he flips through the channels. He finds a home improvement show and sets the remote down. Picking up his plate, he takes a seat right next to me.

"Oh, you're an HGTV fan?" I tease.

"Hey," he says, pretending to be defensive. "You can learn a lot from this channel."

I laugh and take a bite of my food.

I'm loving this new, relaxed side of my boss. I love that he's comfortable with me now, and that I get more from him than icy stares and one-word answers.

We finish our food, occasionally commenting on what we like about the condo makeover, and what we don't. When the show is over, Merrick grabs our plates and takes them to the kitchen.

When he returns, he sits down next to me again. Only this time, he reaches over and takes my hand, intertwining his fingers with mine. And there he sits, watching TV and holding my hand, like it's the most natural thing in the world.

I turn my attention to the TV as well, and smile. I could *definitely* get used to this.

***

The evening is over all too soon, and before I know it I'm at the door ready to leave. I slip into my coat and turn to Merrick.

"Thanks for inviting me to stay."

"Thanks for cooking."

I laugh. "It was my pleasure."

"You can cook for me anytime."

"Is that another invitation?" I ask, with a flirty smile.

He pulls me in for a hug. "Absolutely."

I hold onto him, cherishing the moment. But when I draw back to end the hug, he doesn't let go.

I know it's coming, so my eyes slide closed just before his lips touch mine. It's a sweet kiss, warm and promising.

Stepping back, he whispers, "I'll see you tomorrow."

I just nod at him, unable to speak, my lips still tingling from the kiss. I walk out the door and head to my car, already counting down the hours until I see him again.

* * *

The rest of the week is very much the same. We end the work day and eat dinner together. Except for Wednesday, when I tell him I have mid-week service at church. I take a chance and invite him. He declines, but he doesn't seem angry that I asked him.

It does, however, open up the door for us to talk more about spiritual things. Instead of assuming—which is what I normally do—I openly ask questions. He appreciates my honest interest, and in turn, honestly answers.

Near the end of the week I learn that he grew up in church. I tell him I'm not surprised—I remember the picture I found in the office that day. I see a little hurt in his face when he admits that he misses it.

I just listen. I've been praying for him every day, and I know that God's been doing a slow work in his heart. I can't believe the difference in his willingness to actually have a conversation about it now. I try not to react to anything negative he has to say, and I answer all his questions to the best of my knowledge.

On Friday, he takes me out to dinner. When we pull into Little Mexico's parking lot, I smile.

Remembering the cute elderly lady that gave Merrick so much attention the last time we were here, I can't help but tease him. "Here to see your girlfriend?"

He parks, but before he gets out of the car, he turns to me. "Actually, I *brought* my girlfriend."

My heart stops. Literally.

Okay, it's still beating, but this moment just *begs* for a bit of drama.

Chapter 31

Smiling, I whisper, "Really?"

He reaches over and squeezes my hand. "Really."

Keeping my cool, I step out of the car and close the door. I fall into step beside him, and as we enter the restaurant I act totally normal.

However, my inner Anne is squealing.

Chapter 32

The ball is today.

I spin around one more time in front of the full-length mirror in my bedroom. I hardly recognize myself.

After getting it altered a bit, my blue dress is perfect. My shoes—blue heels with sparkly embellishments around the ankle strap—are surprisingly comfortable. My hair is in a modernized bun at the nape of my neck, with a few tendrils softly hanging down around my face. It's vintage, but still gorgeous. I'm wearing a small silver necklace with a tiny blue sapphire heart hanging from it, and a beautiful pair of diamond earrings.

I love my simple and elegant look.

"Billie? They're going to be here any minute!" Anne calls from the living room. She must've just let herself in. "Are you ready?"

The guys are picking us up together—Prescott and Anne's idea. I grab my small clutch purse, flip the light off, and head out of the room.

"Hi. I'm ready."

"Girl." Anne makes me twirl. "You are breathtaking."

"Uh, right back at ya," I say, my eyes wide. Anne looks like an old-fashioned movie star. Her blond hair is falling down in waves, and her red dress—also altered perfectly—is as beautiful as I remember. Her red lipstick gives her a "classic beauty" look.

"Wow," she says, a huge smile spreading over her face. "The guys are gonna

Chapter 32

pass out when they see us."

We both laugh.

Right on cue, I hear the buzzer and I walk over to hit the button to let them in the building.

"Well," I say, taking a deep breath. "Here they are."

Anne looks like she's going to jump out of her skin as she opens my apartment door.

Prescott steps in, followed by Merrick. I've never seen two better-looking men.

Prescott is in his dress uniform and looks like he should be the poster boy for the Marines. He leans down and kisses Anne on the cheek, telling her how beautiful she is. Just when I think her smile can't get any bigger—it does.

And Merrick. *Oh. My. Word.* I practically lose my breath when he steps toward me. He's in a black tux, with a crisp white shirt and black bow tie. His hair is perfect. He smells perfect. He's just... *perfect*.

He walks over to me and bends slightly, placing a warm kiss to my cheek. His lips linger just for a second, but it's long enough to make me tingle to my toes. I tip my head back, looking up at him.

"You look incredible," I breathe.

He leans back down. I feel his warm breath against my ear as he says, "Incredible doesn't even *begin* to describe the way *you* look."

"You two are stinkin' adorable," Anne giggles.

I feel my face heat up as Merrick steps back and takes my hand.

"You look beautiful, Billie," Prescott offers, smiling.

"Thanks," I say. "And you'll be the best looking Marine at the ball."

I feel Merrick's hand stiffen a bit, but he says nothing.

"Coat?" he asks. "We should get going."

Both Anne and I have warm wraps to wear, and the guys help us into them. Locking the door behind us, we head outside.

I hear Anne squeal before I see it.

"Prescott, it's gorgeous!"

My eyes follow her gaze to the black SUV limo in front of our building.

"We've got a long drive ahead of us," Prescott says, shrugging. "We might as well be comfortable."

I glance at Merrick and his eyes are locked on me. I smile, and he nods.

The guys help us into the limo, and once we're seated comfortably, the driver heads toward Battle Creek.

* * *

"I knew we were supposed to get flurries, but it's coming down pretty hard." Prescott is looking up through the sunroof.

We've been driving for forty-five minutes, and I've noticed the same thing. Snow. A *lot* of snow.

"Good thing we left so early," Merrick says.

Traffic is still moving—just a little slower. We should still be there on time. I sit back with my sparkling grape juice and try to relax.

"This is excitingly romantic," Anne says. "We're going to a military ball just before Christmas, and it's turning into a winter wonderland out there." She sighs and leans back in her seat. "So romantic," she repeats.

I stifle a giggle as the guys look at her like she's lost her mind. Well, Merrick does, anyway. Prescott has this sort of dreaminess in his eyes when he looks at her. It makes me happy, because it's different from the way he looked at me. I can tell he really likes her.

Anne had filled me in on how their coffee date went. I think she used the word "amazing" over a dozen times. She's already head-over-heels, but Anne is like that. Anything she feels is extreme but genuine. I've gotten used to her whimsical spirit, but it takes most people a while to adjust. In all honesty, though, I wouldn't have her any other way.

Merrick reaches over and takes my hand. "Are you excited to see the fruits of our labor?"

I nod. "After all that work, I hope I can enjoy myself and not worry about all the little details."

"We've planned; others will execute tonight."

"I know, I know. I just can't help it."

Chapter 32

He squeezes my hand. "Try not to think about it. Everything was fine when we left the hall yesterday. We've done all we can."

I sigh and look out the window, enjoying the feel of my hand in his larger, warmer one. The snow is *really* coming down now. I feel slightly nervous, and suddenly I remember something.

"Merrick, we have to drive my car home."

"That's right," he says, as if he, too, just remembered.

We had so many things to bring to the hall for setup yesterday that he drove his SUV and I followed in my car—both vehicles packed to the brim. When we were finished, I was so exhausted that we left my car and he drove us both home. It was a good thing, too, because I was asleep within fifteen minutes of getting into the car.

We'd just planned on letting Prescott and Anne have the ride home to themselves.

"I'll drive. We'll be fine," he assures me, putting his arm around my shoulders with a gentle squeeze.

I nod, knowing that we can take our time driving home.

Finally, we're pulling up to the hall. It's absolutely gorgeous on the outside. The inside is even more stunning, from what I remember, and that's without the lights and food and people.

Suddenly, Merrick asks the driver to stop—right in front of where my car is parked. He asks me for my keys. I'm a little confused, but I take them out of my purse and give them to him. He tells me he'll be right back, then he steps out of the limo.

I look at Anne and Prescott, who both innocently shake their heads like they have no idea what's going on.

A moment later I hear the beep of my car being locked, and Merrick is back in the limo, telling the driver to drive to the doors. He hands me my keys.

Um, okay.

The limo pulls up to the front entrance and the driver gets out to open our doors. Being escorted in by the two handsomest men there makes Anne and me swell with pride. We grin at each other, and I have a feeling that with or without all this snow, tonight is going to be magical.

* * *

Whatever I was imagining—this is so much more. Adding the candles, food, and people *does* make a huge difference.

The men are as polished as can be, their uniforms perfection. The women are dazzling in their dresses. They all seem enthusiastic about the theme; some of them are wearing vintage ball gowns, others have hairstyles from the era. But there's one thing everyone has in common—they're all smiling.

I notice Anne looking around the room in awe. "You guys did this?"

I shrug. "Yeah."

"I've never seen anything like it. It's... it's... I don't even have the words," she laughs.

"I'll take that as a compliment."

"You should, Miss Sterling." I turn to Merrick at the sound of my formal name, and there's a bit of humor in his eye.

"Why, thank you, Mr. Anderson, *sir*."

He gives me a devastating smile, and my pulse skips.

"Oh, look!" Anne is pointing to some of our cutouts.

They do look pretty great. Even though they're black and white, the colors of the lights bouncing off them seem to bring them to life.

The live orchestra fills the air with melody. Playing timeless Christmas waltzes, they're adding their own magic into the atmosphere.

We make our way to the food tables, and I smile when I see the bowls of tobacco and plum pudding. It's sparking conversation all over the room.

One of Merrick's ideas was to print off a shortened version of the Christmas Truce on beautiful, old-fashioned parchment paper for the guests to read. As I look around, I see many holding the paper, reading it with delight.

The boys' choir is here and ready, but they won't be singing until later. They're waiting down the hall in a room with kid-friendly snacks and games.

"May I escort you through the receiving line?" Prescott asks. The question

Chapter 32

is directed at the three of us, but it's Anne he offers his arm to.

We agree and follow him.

The next hour and a half is filled with new experiences, from the toast at dinner, to the beautiful ceremony for the retiring sergeant major. I'll admit, I get a little teary-eyed more than once. Especially hearing the boys' choir sing "O Holy Night" in German.

Overall, the celebration is absolutely fascinating.

But my favorite part of the evening is when Merrick asks me to dance. I feel as though I've entered one of the fairy tales I read as a girl. I had no idea he could dance, but every part of my being was hoping he would ask me.

I follow him to the dance floor where the other couples are already dancing, and we find a space off to the side. The orchestra is playing Frank Sinatra's "The Christmas Waltz". He takes my hand in his and begins to lead.

"I wasn't sure you could dance," I say, truthfully.

"You don't run a business like mine without learning how to dance," he answers, smiling. "The majority of events I plan include dancing."

"You're great at it."

He smiles, not taking his eyes off mine.

We dance for a few moments in silence, and I'm trying to permanently burn every moment into my memory—the music I hear, the fragrances I smell, the arms I feel around me...

Yes, I think it's safe to say the evening is pretty near perfect.

* * *

As the end of the evening draws near, I excuse myself to the ladies' room, knowing it's a long ride home. I'm gone longer than expected, because I run into a little trouble with my dress. Wishing Anne had come to the restroom with me, I do my best to straighten it all out.

When I finally make it back to the table, Anne has a funny look on her face.

"Where's Merrick?" I ask.

"Uh, some woman came to the table just after you left, asking to speak with him privately." She shrugs, hesitating before the next part. "He walked away with her and hasn't been back."

Weird. I wonder if there's some sort of trouble with something we organized. I'm hoping I didn't make a stupid mistake that will reflect badly on him and his business.

"I'll see if I can find him," I say, fighting a yawn. The day is starting to catch up with me.

I walk out of the huge hall, heading down a hallway where I saw some open rooms earlier. Even if he's meeting with someone important, at least I'll know where he went off to.

I peek in a few empty rooms before I find him. And when I find him, I nearly lose my ability to speak.

There, in one of several open but empty rooms, stands Merrick with a woman.

A woman he's embracing with the same arms that held me moments ago during our last waltz.

A woman I instantly recognize as Sophia Denmark.

Chapter 33

I back away slowly, hoping they don't notice me. When I'm out of the room, I turn and nearly run back to the ballroom. Fighting tears, I'm determined to act like nothing's wrong as I approach our table. I can't handle answering any questions right now.

People are twirling and waltzing around me, but I pay them no mind as I spot Prescott and Anne. I make my way to the table and grab my clutch.

Anne—who knows me almost as well as I know myself—immediately asks me what's wrong.

I shake my head. "Nothing," I say, trying to sound casual. "I'm not feeling well. I need to go."

Prescott stands. "I'll get Merrick. He can—"

"No," I say quickly. "Tell him I took my car. I hope you don't mind him being the third wheel on your way home."

My attempt at a joke doesn't go over well, and Anne frowns.

"Billie, you're upset. You don't need to be driving for the next hour and a half—*especially* not in this weather."

"Anne," I say with a bit of warning in my voice. "Please let me go. I'll call you tomorrow."

She looks a bit stunned as I grab my wrap and walk away. But neither her nor Prescott follow me, so I'm satisfied that my tone has had the desired effect.

When I step outside, I'm met with an icy blast to my face. Not only is the snow still coming down steadily, but the wind is making it seem a lot more menacing. Walking carefully, I head to my car.

About twenty steps in, my feet are numb. I didn't even think to bring boots with me. I just keep telling myself that in a moment I'll be able to blast the heat right onto my toes.

I finally reach my car and start it. Thankfully, the snow is still powdery and soft, so it doesn't take me long to brush it off the windows.

I sit in the car for a moment, letting it warm up. "Lord," I say out loud. I look up through the windshield. "I can't handle this. Not now."

For the first time since I walked around that corner, I allow myself to think about what I saw.

My boyfriend, embracing his ex-girlfriend. In a room. A *private* room.

A few tears fall as I back out of my parking space. I know I'm being a bit dramatic, but with everything that's been going on, my emotions still haven't gotten off the roller coaster. This was just an unexpected hill and drop. Straight down.

Pulling out of the parking lot and onto the main road, I glance at the clock. 9:38. I decide that I can make this drive. It may take me three hours, but there's nowhere I'd rather be than home, having myself a good cry.

Gripping the steering wheel, I set a slow and steady pace. I'm a bit nervous to drive in this weather, but I'm even more anxious to be home. I flip the radio on low and listen to Christmas music, hoping it will help keep me calm.

Then I let the tears flow.

* * *

It's about 10:15 when I realize I don't have my phone. I had set it on the seat next to me in the limo after taking a selfie with Merrick. I forgot to put it back in my purse. It's a good thing that I remember the way home, because if I needed my GPS, I'd be out of luck right now.

I know Anne will see my phone and grab it for me. I just hope she doesn't

Chapter 33

panic if she tries to call and doesn't get an answer.

Oh, well. I'm too far into the drive to turn back now.

I begin to relax after realizing that I'm pretty much the only one on the road right now. I can take my time and focus on the road ahead instead of traffic around me.

I've been on the road about an hour when I see the F-250 coming up behind me. It's no big deal—I'll just pull over and let them pass, like I have been. I'm on a two-way freeway, and I don't want to hold him up. Besides, he's probably way more confident in that huge truck than I am in my tiny car.

I flip on my hazards and pull slowly onto the shoulder to wait until he passes. I get a bit nervous, however, when I see how fast he's approaching. *He'd better slow down. He's going to cause a wreck!*

I just finish the thought when I feel him clip the corner of my back bumper. My car jolts violently from the impact. Almost involuntarily, I cry out. I'm white-knuckling the steering wheel as my car is spinning. Pumping the brakes doesn't help.

"Oh, God, help me!" I feel myself headed downhill. It's one of those times where before you can tell yourself not to panic, panic has already set up camp.

When my car finally stops, I breathe a sigh of relief, thankful there wasn't a crash. I've completely stopped moving. It's completely dark, so I flip on the light above my head. Trying to look out, all I can see is white. Every window—white. I turn the wipers to the highest setting to clear the mounds of snow that have settled on the windshield. Still, I see only white.

I groan. *"Great."*

I look down at my attire. Ball gown and high heels. Dear Lord, could I be in a worse situation?

I decide to bite the bullet and get out of the car. A few moments in the cold won't be so bad, as long as I can see what kind of situation I'm in.

Only... I can't open the door. I push and push, but it doesn't budge.

"Ooooh, I am *so* not dressed for this," I say to myself as I climb into the passenger seat. I try that door. Stuck.

"Are you *kidding* me?" I'm even more frustrated now, if that's possible. Reaching between my legs, I grab the front and back of my long skirt and tie a knot. Makeshift pants. But I don't have time to be proud of myself. I climb between the front seats and nearly fall into the back seat. I try both doors. No luck.

I sit for a moment, trying to think. The windows. Still in the back seat, I try the driver's side window. It goes down, and snow falls in.

"Ah!" I yell, brushing it off. Then I reach my hand through the open window—or try to, at least. It's a wall of snow.

"What in the world?" I try to punch through, but it's solid.

Quickly, I check all the other windows, not caring about how much snow I'm letting in. I get the same result.

"Oh… my… gosh. I'm literally trapped in this car!" I'm yelling to myself, but somehow, speaking out loud makes me feel less alone.

I go to grab my purse when I remember: I have no phone.

I collapse back into the seat, feeling defeated. No one knows where I am. I don't have a phone. I can't get out of my vehicle.

I look up. "Father, show me what to do. I'm not even going to lie—I'm scared. Help me trust You."

I climb awkwardly back into the driver seat. I sit for a moment, trying to think and not panic. At least I can be thankful that my car is still running, and that I have heat and a light. For now.

I'm looking around the car for anything that might spark an idea, when something catches my eye. On the floor of the passenger side is a box. A gift, to be exact. I reach over and pick it up.

The gift is square, a little bigger than a box of tissue, and wrapped beautifully. The paper is red and gold, and the gold is shimmery. There's a sparkly red bow on top. There's a card taped to the bottom. It says "Miss Sterling."

I recognize my boss's handwriting. So this is what he put in my car when we first pulled into the parking lot.

I'm struck with a bitter thought. This gift was given before his run-in with *her*. Ugh.

Chapter 33

Then I tell myself to stop being a baby. I could kick myself for running off like I did. Not only am I in this situation because of it, but also I wasn't being fair. I don't know what happened and I never gave him the chance to explain.

Suddenly, I feel very foolish. Why did I let my emotions run wild? Why do I always assume the worst? Sure, it could've been bad, but I didn't stay long enough to find out.

I rest my head against the steering wheel and squeeze my eyes shut. "Oh, I *so* need a behavioral makeover. What have you done, Billie?"

Sitting back up, I stare at the box in my hand. A part of me wants to wait to open it until he's with me and I've heard his side of the story. But the other—more dramatic—part wants to open it before I die.

Hey. It's a very real possibility.

I pull the card from the gift and open it. It's got a little snowman waving on the front. Cute. I open it.

Billie,

I know this holiday will be extremely difficult for you. I want you to know that I am here.

Always.

Love, Merrick.

I can barely make out his name through the tears. I set the card aside and tear open the paper. I don't immediately see the gift—it's in a plain white box.

Opening the top, I reach inside. I feel something smooth and round. I pull it out and suck in a breath.

It's a beautiful clear glass pumpkin. And there, in the center, is a picture of me and my dad. Merrick must've gotten it from my social media page. It's one of my favorites. It was taken about a year and a half ago, when my dad still looked healthy. I'm sitting on the edge of his knee with my arm around his shoulders, and we're both laughing.

Tears are running in a steady stream down my face now. This was so thoughtful. And for him to remember Dad's nickname for me and use it as a frame—that just put it over the top.

I sit, clutching the glass pumpkin to my chest, and cry. I don't even know how long I sit there. I just know I need this right now.

Every emotion makes its way down my face in the form of salty tears. My chest is soaked with them now, but I don't care.

Finally, I look up, and in a desperate plea, pray, "Lord, let him find me."

Chapter 34

It's after midnight. I start my car again, blasting the heat. I've been turning my car off every so often, sitting here in the dark and silence for as long as I can stand the cold. There's not even room for me to move around and try to get warm.

I've read my card from Merrick over and over, and the glass pumpkin is sitting on the dashboard. In a weird way, it's keeping me company.

I turn on the light above my head again and reach for the glove compartment. Popping it open, I dig around until I find what I'm looking for. My tiny, red, pocket New Testament.

Flipping through it, I look for a specific verse—one that I memorized as a kid. Sure, I could quote it, but there's something comforting in opening the Bible and seeing it there in black and white. When I find it, I read out loud: "'For God has not given us a spirit of fear, but of power, love, and a sound mind.' 1 Timothy 1:7."

I read it again and again, letting the words fill the little space in the car.

Then I pray for probably the fiftieth time. "Lord, help me not fear."

I pray this because I *am* afraid. I'm afraid of being left here—wherever I am—and no one finding me. I worry about running out of gas and freezing. I'm terrified that I'll never see the man I love again…

"Oh. My. Gosh. I *do* love him," I say out loud.

The tears start all over again. That's why it hurt so much. It wasn't just *any* man holding another woman. It was the man I love holding another woman.

"God, please help me be patient," I sob. "Help me wait for an answer, and not jump to conclusions anymore."

I'm exhausted. I just want to recline in my seat and fall asleep. But I'm cold. And scared. And...

Wait.

I turn and look at the back seat. I can't believe I've forgotten that it folds down. I scramble over my own seat and land hard on my shoulder. Oh, well. This is no time to worry about a little pain.

I grab the little flap at the top and yank the seat down, probably a little too hard. Well, I'm excited. I can't help it.

I can see into my trunk. There's my gray blanket I keep for emergencies. I pull it out and wrap it around my legs. Oh, I could've used this hours ago. Feeling around some of the junk I keep in the back of my car, I search for my flashlight. Bingo. I click it on.

Reaching back over the driver seat, I turn off the engine and stick my keys in the front of my dress. Hey, it's what you do when you don't have pockets. Then I stretch my arm to push the trunk button. I hear the pop and almost laugh. I turn back to the trunk.

Lying on my back, I slide myself in headfirst. Then I carefully push up. The trunk opens, letting in a blast of snow. I'm so happy, I don't even care. I push the trunk open all the way and sit up.

I suck in a deep breath. My mind knows I haven't been suffocating, but I don't think my body believes it. I breathe in the cold air like I've been out of oxygen for the last few hours.

Using my flashlight, I try to see where I am. From what I can tell, my car has landed in a huge ditch, wedging itself like a hot dog in a bun. That's why I couldn't open the doors or get out the windows.

I know I'm going to have to climb out, and I'm dreading it. I wish I had boots. I turn the flashlight back to the trunk and look around for something—anything—I can use.

There are quite a few things back here, but no ideas are coming to me.

Chapter 34

Until...

I smile. It's perfect.

Picking up an old newspaper that I had thrown in and forgotten about, I begin to take it apart, opening up every page and setting it to the side. Then I see my stash of plastic grocery bags and grab those.

Removing my shoes first, I take the newspaper pages and begin to wrap them around my feet and up my calves. I do this on both legs until the newspaper is gone. Then I begin putting the plastic grocery bags over the newspaper, tying them as high up my leg as I can. I tie five bags on each foot.

Now I've got boots.

I laugh. They're not very pretty (okay, they're hideous), but they are fairly comfortable. And they'll keep my feet dry. Surrounded by my warm wrap and my fleece blanket, I carefully step out of the car.

Oh. Lord. It's cold. I shake off the thought and focus. Patting the front of my dress, I make sure I have the keys before I close the trunk. Then I climb on top of the car and begin waving my flashlight.

* * *

It's a miracle. It has to be. Not one car has passed in what seems like forever, and the one pulling up now is a black SUV limo.

I can't help it—I start crying.

The limo doesn't even come to a complete stop before the door bursts open and Merrick jumps out.

"Billie!"

I'm sobbing too hard to answer, but he's down in the ditch and on my car in less than ten seconds. I'm shivering as he scoops me up, crushing me to him.

"How did you find me?" I manage to say through my chattering teeth.

"I prayed, Billie. I prayed that God would lead me to you, and He did." He squeezes me harder. "He did."

"You... you prayed?" Oh, we are *so* talking about this later.

"Billie!"

I whip my head to the side. "Anne!"

Prescott and Anne are standing at the top of the ditch, and Prescott is reaching for me.

"Give her to me."

"I got her," Merrick says, his grip on me not loosening even a bit. "Just help me out."

Prescott helps pull Merrick out with me in his arms. In just a moment, we're all climbing into the limo. When Prescott and Anne jump in the front, I look at Merrick questioningly.

He shrugs. "I may have paid the driver to let us use this for the night so he could go home." He hesitates. "I paid for his cab, too."

"So, Prescott is driving?"

"Yeah."

I'm quiet a moment, then say, "Uh, are you going to let me go?" He's still holding me, only now we're in the seat and I'm on his lap.

"No."

I laugh.

He demands to know what happened, and I tell him every detail as Prescott and Anne listen from the front. When I get to the part about making my own boots, he smiles at me.

"You're so smart."

I blush. "Thanks." Then a thought hits me. "How did you know I didn't make it home?"

His face is hard. "We left right after you. Anne found your phone in here, so we knew we couldn't call you. When we passed the spot where you were, we didn't see you because it was so dark. We made it home, but I asked the driver to stop at your apartment first."

"And I wasn't there," I say softly.

He shakes his head. "I nearly went crazy with worry. That's when we made a deal with the driver, so we could take the limo. I didn't want to waste any time going home to get my car."

"So, you drove all the way back to the ball?"

"Yeah. I wanted to retrace your tire tracks. I knew we had missed

Chapter 34

something in the dark."

"Thank you for not giving up on me," I whisper.

Suddenly, he calls to the front. "Prescott. Window."

I see Prescott nod, then the little privacy window between driver and rider closes. We're pretty much alone now.

I turn to face him, and his look is serious.

"Why did you leave the ball?"

"I… I saw you…" The words stick in my throat.

"You saw me with Sophia."

I nod.

"I'm so sorry," he says, pressing his forehead to mine. "I wish I could've explained."

I nod, fighting tears again. "I know. That was my fault. I just—"

"Stop, Billie. It's not all your fault. I handled the situation badly. I should've told you she'd be there."

"You knew?" I ask, my eyes widening.

"Yeah. I knew. Remember the day she called my office?"

I nod again.

"She wanted to get together—do lunch or something. I refused. Finally, she mentioned that she had heard about the ball, and that she'd find a way to go. She knew some of the Marines that would be attending." He pauses, looking toward the window. "I guess I didn't take her seriously."

"But she came," I whisper.

"She came," he agrees.

"I didn't see her."

"I think she pretty much stayed out of sight, for our sake."

My eyebrows rise.

"I told her over the phone that I was seeing someone." He shrugs. "I think she was trying to respect that."

"Um, I'm a little confused," I say, and he laughs.

"Billie, she waited until you weren't there to approach me. I think she didn't want you to feel threatened."

I cross my arms. "I'm not threatened."

Merrick kisses me softly. "You shouldn't be."

I lift my chin in an overly confident manner. "Continue."

"She asked to speak with me privately, so I followed her to a room down the hall. Once we got there, she started to cry."

"Oh?" I say. "Pining away for you, was she?"

Merrick grins. "Not exactly. She wanted to apologize."

I shift on his lap and look directly at him. "Apologize?"

"Yep. She told me that she's given her life completely to the Lord, and she's moving to Colorado with her family. Her dad will be pastoring there."

"Really?" My voice sounds small.

"Really. And she told me that God had been dealing with her to make things right with me before she left. She seemed truly sorry, Billie. I told her I forgive her. Then she hugged me."

Feeling foolish, I look away. "That's what I saw."

He wraps his arms around me and pulls me close. "I'm so sorry, Billie. I know what it must've looked like."

Suddenly very tired, I lay my head on his shoulder. "I thought she wanted you back."

"Even if she did," he says, his voice low in my ear, "I would've told her I'm in love with someone else."

I lift my head up and look at him. "You love me?"

He answers me with a kiss.

When we break apart, he says, "There's something else, Billie."

"Hmm?"

"I'm done running."

"Running?" I whisper, but I know where this is going. My pulse speeds up.

"When Prescott was driving back to the hall, I had a lot of time to myself back here to think. And… pray."

I smile.

"My life has never been the same since I quit going to church and started running from God." He frowns. "In fact, it's been miserable."

"Good," I tease.

He grins and continues. "The truth is, you've opened my eyes to what a

Chapter 34

fool I've been, thinking I could live my life without Him."

"I've been praying for you. So much."

He squeezes me. "I know. Thank you."

Suddenly the weight of what he's saying hits me. "Oh my gosh. This is amazing. Will you come to church with me?"

"Of course. I can't wait—I miss it."

"I'm so happy," I say. Then I look at him. "You're sure there's nothing between you and Sophia anymore? You know, now that you both are... back on the right track?"

He gently cups my chin and makes me look at him. "Billie, there are no feelings there, except the ones that wish her well and hope for the best in her future."

I'm satisfied with his answer. "Okay," I say, happily.

"Besides, there's not a person on this earth who I'd rather have working for me. I don't want any other woman bothering me at my desk, or throwing away my sticky notes, or trying to make me laugh with her mock salutes."

A grin spreads over my face. "Hey," I say, feigning irritation. "I know you're laughing on the inside."

He pulls me close for a kiss. "You're right," he murmurs against my lips. "I guess I need to laugh out loud more often."

I sit up, laughing. "Couldn't hurt. Oh!" I say, remembering something.

He tips his head in question.

"My gift," I breathe.

"You opened it?"

"Uh, yeah," I say, as if it should be obvious. "What else was I to do, trapped in that car for hours and hours?" I kiss the tip of his nose. "I love it. So much."

He looks at me, and it seems like he's searching for something in my eyes. Finally, he just says, "I love you, Billie Sterling."

I smile, and it feels like my heart is going to burst. "I love you too, sir."

He laughs, and I love the sound.

Epilogue

I said yes.

To what, you may ask?

To Merrick's Christmas proposal, of course.

It. Was. Beautiful.

He invited me to spend Christmas in Pennsylvania with him and his family. Knowing what a tough Christmas this would be (the first one without my dad), I gratefully accepted.

His parents—Joseph and Patricia—were over the moon about us coming. They fixed up their spare room for me—complete with apple cinnamon wax melts. Gee, I have no idea how they found out about my love for all things cinnamon and spice. *Wink, wink.*

Merrick was a perfect gentleman and took the couch in the family room.

It was a great way to spend Christmas. I baked cookies with Patricia, helped with Christmas dinner, and just enjoyed the time spent with them.

Both of his parents were ecstatic about Merrick rededicating his life to Jesus. They both cried and let him know how long they had prayed for him.

More than once, Patricia hugged me with tears in her eyes and told me how thankful she was that Merrick found me. I felt humbled and blessed.

But the true shining moment of the holiday was when Merrick handed me that little red box on Christmas Eve. When I opened it, a yellow sticky-note popped out that simply said "Marry me". Under the note was a beautiful engagement ring.

You know how I answered. And yes, there most *definitely* was an Anne squeal.

Now, as we sit here on the plane, flying home, we chat about the when.

"I don't want to wait," Merrick says, squeezing my hand.

"I don't either," I agree.

"January?"

"You think we can pull it off?"

He grins. "Planning is what I do best, Miss Sterling."

"You know, you won't be able to call me that for much longer." I give him a know-it-all smile.

"That's why I'm going to use the name as much as I can now," he teases.

I playfully jab his rib. "Look at you, joking around. Why, it seems like only a few months ago, you were shooting me daggers with your eyes and freezing the room with your mere presence."

"And it seems like only yesterday you were dropping papers and tripping up the steps."

"That *was* yesterday," I deadpan.

He leans over, kissing my temple. "Some things never change."

"And some things *do* change," I say, placing my hand on his cheek. "And I, for one, am so thankful."